THE Fall

(Book Two)

Thou Shall Not Hide

By

Sabrina B. Scales

Copyright 2020 Sabrina B. Scales

All rights reserved.

Cover Art: Jacob Lund/Adobe Stock

Dedication

This one is dedicated to 2019 and the many great experiences it brought. To every reader who took a chance and read my stories for the first time, and especially those who traveled to book signings and brought nothing but love to my table. For every soul who selflessly promoted my work simply for the love of the craft. To my fellow authors who I've watched watering, blossoming and growing, I see you. I love you. I wish you nothing but the best. To those I loved who didn't make it into the year 2020, you will be missed and reflected in every word I write. To my husband who has watched me sit in front of this computer making up sh*t and convincing folks to read it, thanks for not dropping me off at the psych ward! I love you real big!

Description

Even the saved struggle when navigating their way through love. This much could definitely be said for the Fold Family's youngest child and only son, Chadwick.

Looking for love was never on Chad's list of things to do until he held Taya in his arms on a dance floor and watched God laugh at his plans. She was beautiful in a way that caught his eyes and his heart. Foreign feelings that wouldn't fade had him questioning his sanity.

They're both too young to fathom that any of this could be real. So, they come and go then come back again until there's nowhere left to hide.

Take this journey of discovering, uncovering, and everything in between in this story of love defined in the second installment of The Fold!

One

"Even with full understanding of all that is at stake,

the flesh can be powerless under the spirit of temptation.

But when you find her, she'll be more than a lover.

More than flesh and temptation.

She'll be the salt of your ministry, bringing meaning to it all."

-Pops-

Distractions.

That's all women were to me. Something to keep my eyes and hands busy until I got back to work. Sometimes they lasted hours. And the more ambitious ones who wanted to land a permanent seat next to me at my father's church, might even last through the night. But at the end of it all, that's all they were.

Distractions.

Nothing more and nothing less.

The distraction for the night was Rachel, a long-haired redbone with more legs than conversation, who'd fallen asleep

1

next to me after a round or two or three. She lucked up and grabbed my attention after another woman left me with nothing to show for our chance encounter but a picture that blew up on Instagram and flooded DMs with questions from random strangers about who I was and invites to do interviews with Boom Central.

Speaking of which, let me touch on that for a minute. Because Taya, the fine ass, singing ass, lead vocalist for The Crew, a group my boy Sabre was a part of, was the reason for the five minutes of fame that I didn't want and hadn't asked for. We ran into each other at a co-ed bachelor party me and Sabre were throwing for our homeboy Keith. It'd been a minute since we had time to link up since life had sent us in different directions with Keith joining the Army, me opening a tattoo parlor, and Sabre joining a supergroup under the label of one of Houston's most influential artists, platinum rapper, Plus. It was an added bonus that he brought a couple of his bandmates along, cornbread fed Bre and the sweetheart of the group, Taya. The two others, Jock and Kimi Wells couldn't make it due to stomach viruses. And honestly, I wasn't concerned with all that. I wished them well, but that was about it.

What I *was* concerned with was how damn sexy Taya looked in person. Five feet and at least eight inches of just the kinda woman I was after. Dressed in a pair of black leather pants and a sleeveless spandex top that showed peeps of the sides of her breasts, the girl was practically screaming for me to grovel at her feet. Don't get me wrong, Bre was bad. But there was something about Taya that made everything around her disappear. I was sweating under my arms, nervous for no reason. Even the music turned down when she walked into our section. I could barely grasp the concept of breathing.

Damn.

"Hey! You must be Chad." She yelled over the music. And even her speaking voice sounded like a song as she approached me, sitting in a huge VIP booth that we'd reserved for our party of twenty.

"I *am*," I yelled back, nodding and standing from my seat, taking her hand and pulling it up to my lips for a kiss. "Nice to meet you, Miss Maxey." I gave a cocky smile that had been known to melt the panties off of many women.

"*Miss Maxey's* my mama." She corrected, giving a slanted smile of her own. "You can call me Taya." She leaned her head to the side, pretty brown eyes catching flickers of the strobe light.

"Might be hard to call you at all without a phone number." I wasn't with pumping brakes. It was obvious she was feeling me seeing as she'd made it through a sea of niggas and landed right in front of me.

"Slow down, Mister Fold." Her smile widened, pearly white teeth glowing beneath full glossed lips that I was willing to bet tasted like champagne. "We got all night for that. Can we at least dance first?" She hiked a brow, so sexy and so damn forward. Luckily for her, I was with that shit. Forward was my favorite direction.

Lyrics from a throwback, Fantasia's *"Falling In Love Tonight"* came blaring through the speakers, and I took that as an omen from the Lord himself, to take Taya by the hand that I'd just kissed and lead her onto the dance floor. I could feel eyes on us, half of them belonging to the bridal party that didn't even have a chance to ask for an autograph before I'd stolen her away. All the nervous energy running wild in my chest turned into nuts or courage, or something similar to it. And before either of us knew it, we were pressed together with my hands around her waist and her fingers locked together at the back of my neck.

A pair of metallic red bottoms put her lips right at my nose, a dangerous proximity for someone who smelled and looked so good. Her hair was pulled up in a bun on top of her head, a strip of diamonds hung from each of her ears, sparkling against mahogany skin. My hungry palms followed the sway of her hips, trying hard not to feel her up out of respect for who she was. Fast tempos weren't usually my speed, but a slow song wouldn't've been a good idea. Looking down into her eyes, I felt an intoxication that had nothing to do with the four shots I'd taken. Her body was warm, lower back curving into the palm of my hand as I temporarily lost my composure and caressed the skin that was completely exposed from the rise of her hips all the way up to the landing of her breasts. I could've stayed out there all night, holding her, feeling her, grinning like a teenaged boy when she giggled as my lips grazed her neck. She had me singing and feeling light, forgetting all my usual intentions. And as we heard the song ending, I wished I had a remote to press repeat.

"You good?" She applied pressure to the back of my neck, forcing my head down low enough for her to whisper in my ear.

"Yeah. Why'd you ask?" I leaned back, brows scrunched as she stared up into my eyes with concern that didn't seem necessary.

That is unless she was reading my mind and knew that I was having a damned out of body experience. That my draw to her had gone from something physical to something that I couldn't put into words.

"You just looked... I don't know. Like you left." She tried explaining, having no idea how accurate she was.

"Nah, I'm right here." I squeezed her tighter. "I know you feel me!" I leaned in and grazed her earlobe with my mouth, causing her to giggle and tighten her hold around my neck as we kept on dancing to the next song on rotation.

It was easier when we were closer. No room for eye contact and the opportunity for her to read me. I didn't need that any more than I needed a hole in my head. What I needed was for somebody to come turn off this voodoo.

"Awe shit! Lemme find out you finding love in the club!" Bre came out of nowhere in the nick of time, with Sabre close behind looking like a big brother.

Taya smiled and rolled her eyes, bringing them right back to me. Then that feeling quickly resurfaced and my heart started skipping beats.

"You sure you're okay?" She asked again.

Was this woman psychic or was I the one tripping?

"I swear, I'm good. You a nurse or somethin'?"

"No." She shook her head. "But your eyes..."

"They always look like that. It's part of my appeal." I winked and that seemed to suffice for the duration of our dance. All was well aside from the mini heart attack taking place in my chest, and then the infamous picture was taken by Bre before we all headed off the floor.

After hanging back at the booth with us for a little bit, Taya, Bre, and Sabre cut out due to early rehearsals the next morning. I felt empty as hell without Taya sitting next to me, even though Rachel had swooped in before she even made it out the door. It was crazy, the thought of missing somebody that you'd only known for a few hours. But I chalked it up to drinking on an empty stomach. My sister told me that shit was gonna catch up to me one day.

"Good morning." A tall, almond-colored sister with long, fire-red curls hanging down her back pranced into my bathroom while I stood at the sink, brushing my teeth, attempting to drown out my thoughts long enough to figure out how to gracefully put her out of my crib.

"Mornin'." I nodded, hiking my brows at her reflection in the mirror before spitting a mouthful of minty suds into the basin. "You sleep well?" I asked though I wasn't really concerned. I'd only brought her home to distract me from the fact that I was still thinking about Taya.

"Yeah. I was—"

"Cool. I can pay for your Lyft. Where you stayin'?"

I didn't mean to be short, but in my experience, that was the only way to be.

Leave no room for misinterpretation, no matter how good the sex was.

No morning sex allowed.

*And don't even **think** about offering breakfast.*

The only thing that was ever gonna take place between me and this woman was over and done before the sun kissed the sky.

"Damn, that was *rude*." She backed out of the bathroom door and retrieved her dress from the footboard of my bed where she'd abandoned it two minutes after walking into my place. "Brandi said you were an ass."

"Brandi don't even know me." I rinsed, spat and smirked.

"That's the point." Rachel sighed, sitting on the foot of my bed, securing the straps on a pair of bright yellow sandals with heels that had accentuated her long, toned legs both standing *and* bent over my dresser.

"She's been with Keith, what, two years, and is just now meeting his *alleged* best friend one week before their wedding? Ever wondered why?" She slanted a set of almost midnight eyes up at me as I walked into the bedroom with a towel around my waist, skin still dewy from the quick shower I'd just taken.

"Nah, actually, I hadn't given it much thought." I brushed a hand down the stubble on my chin, deciding that it'd be the look for the day because I was too exhausted to shave.

"Well, maybe you should." She stated as if she'd known me more than eight damn hours.

"Where are you staying?" I asked, ignoring her suggestion.

Ignoring *her*.

"Why, you wanna do this again tonight?" I was well on my way to the closet to fetch my Sunday attire but could hear the hopeful smile in her voice.

"Busy day," I yelled back. "But the Lyft will need to know where to drop you off. That is unless you like roaming around strange cities."

"I'll order my own Lyft, Mr. Fold." She said as I reentered the room, tucking a crisp, white dress shirt into my charcoal slacks.

"Suit yourself." I fastened my personalized quill-cufflinks, shrugging and sliding my eyes from her exposed backbone to the mirror mounted over my dresser.

She mumbled something about *preacher's kids being assholes* and how *good dick always came with a headache.* And I successfully tuned her out, rubbing a fingertip full of my sister's handmade shea butter moisturizer in my hands and distributing it evenly through my short locks before footing into my Ferragamos and making my way to the hanging rack beside my bed that housed my extensive cologne collection.

"Do your parents know you're a man-whore?" She'd stood up and located her purse on the nightstand next to her cell.

"Rachel, with all due respect, if this is your way of leaving a lasting impression, you've missed the mark by a mile." I worked half a dime-sized amount of cologne between my wrists.

"Really?" She smirked, weight shifting to one narrow hip as she planted a skinny hand on the other. "And what would be a good way to leave a lasting impression? I mean aside from what I did to you last night?"

I turned completely around to face her, sliding a finger under her sharp chin, taking a second to stare into her eyes as she held her breath in anticipation.

"Last night was amazing." I leaned in close to her thin lips and said. "Damn near perfect, to be honest. And one day, somebody's gonna appreciate that thing you do with your leg behind your head. Seriously." I grinned and she did too, chin still resting on my fingertip like she was scared to pull away.

"But it won't be me." I continued and her whole demeanor slumped. "I'm not the kinda guy who calls the next day. I don't even have your number, nor do I want it. Some things are better left imagined, Rachel. Trust me on this one."

She stood there for a full five seconds after I'd tipped her chin up and retracted my finger. I brushed her elbow in route to the bedroom door, then waited there for her to follow me out of the room. She did so with hesitance, face sagging with disappointment. I'd seen that face enough times to know exactly what it was, and it'd taken years for me to understand that it wasn't my issue to resolve. Whether it had taken a week, five months or five years for a woman to make it to my bed, she made it there knowing that it would be her first and last time. I didn't do riddles, not on paper or in person. At twenty-four, I still had a lot of moves to make, and falling in love wasn't even in the top twenty.

"Guess I'll see you at the wedding, then." Rachel brushed past me, giving me one last look at that tight behind laying unpantied under a slinky dress that had easily given me access to a finger fuck under the table back at Bottoms.

"Later." I held the door open and she walked out, pulling out her phone and ordering her own Lyft.

Perfect.

Didn't cost me a dime.

Nobody could direct the youth choir with as much enthusiasm as my sister, Jada, and that was certainly the case on this particular Sunday. I'd shown up right on time, despite the fatigue ravishing my limbs, and landed a seat right beside our older sister, Angela, respectfully known as Penny, and my little niece Patience, referred to most as Boogie, just as Jada was leaving her seat at the end of the choir stand.

It was a rare occasion to see her up there wearing a robe looking all saved and uniformed. Jada kept up her attendance at church but had fallen into the background as far as the choir ministry was concerned. Now she seemed rejuvenated. Back to herself in so many ways. And we could give a large majority of that glory to God. But at least fifty percent had to be handed to my boy, her new fiancé, Andrew "The Jet" Julian.

"*Chadwick.*" Angela greeted before I could even take my seat. She knew exactly how much I hated my government name and made a point to use it as often as possible.

"Gretchen." I tipped my chin and shot back as usual with the most undesirable name I could muster. Her chuckle let me know that I'd done well in this childish battle that had been going on since I was old enough to talk.

"That's a good one." She nodded, releasing Boogie from her hold so she could scoot closer to me and plant a peppermint-scented kiss on my cheek as she hugged my neck with her tiny little arms.

"Had to reach into the archives. Glad you liked it!" I grinned. "And where's my peppermint, Boogie? I know you ain't gon' let Uncle have funky breath."

"Your breath's not funky, Unkie Chad!" She smiled, cueing up a dimple and a set of brown cheeks that looked exactly like her mama's.

"Is that right?" I slanted my eyes down at her as she tucked into my side.

She nodded *yes*.

"If it's not funky then what does it smell like?" I couldn't help but ask. Boogie always said the most off the wall things and Penny couldn't stand it.

"Boogie, put your headphones on." Penny cut her eyes at me, knowing exactly what I was up to.

"What? She didn't answer me yet." I grinned.

"It smells like kisses." Boogie blurted. "*Girl* kisses!" Her eyes widened as they jotted from me to her mama.

"That's enough, Patience Marie. Put these on *now*." Penny placed a set of bright pink headphones on Boogie's ears and cleared her throat in a threatening manner toward me.

"Man, you a hater." I chuckled, shaking my head. "Niece was about to spit some knowledge. You hate to see it."

"I'd also *hate to see* a knot upside your head." She curved her lips as our sister stood before the youth choir that would be performing under her direction for the first time in years.

"Drew musta really put it down in Tokyo." Penny leaned in

and whispered, abandoning the fact that she'd just basically called me trifling, planting both hands on the sides of Boogie's cushioned headphones to make sure she couldn't hear anything but the educational video she was tuned into while tucked snugly under my arm.

"Can we not do that?" I scrunched my face with disgust.

"What? Talk about your sister gettin' smashed on a private jet? I thought you'd be intrigued." She flashed a sly grin, high cheekbones pushing her eyes into a squint.

"Bruh, do y'all live to make me sick? Like do you wake up in the morning and incorporate it into your daily affirmations?" I asked, glancing down at Boogie who'd already fallen asleep because anything her mama had her watching was automatically boring.

"No. But that's not a bad idea." Angela winked at me before reaching into the backpack beside her and retrieving a blanket to lay over her sleeping baby girl.

"But seriously, it's good to see her back up there." She sighed. "Almost feels like old times, you know?"

"Emphasis on *almost*." I returned, tucking the blanket around Boogie's shoulder in response to her tiny frame shivering against the side of me. "Still a big piece missing." I turned my eyes to my big sister.

She straightened her calf-length navy blue dress as well as her posture, eyes straight ahead as Jada motioned for the altos to do their thing. "Don't start." She said without looking at me. "Don't even *think* about starting that today."

"I'm not startin'. I'm just sayin'." I had to raise my voice as the congregation started shouting in response to semi-high-pitched voices glorifying the Lord.

"It's the same difference, and I'm not in the mood." She rolled her eyes, rubbing a hand down Boogie's arm and clearing her throat as the sopranos took over, swaying side to side with their mouths open as wide as they'd go sending praises straight up to Heaven.

"You got a timer on that?" I asked, involuntarily patting my thigh to the beat.

"On what?"

"Your mood? It's been what, two years?"

"I wasn't counting." She returned, taking a deep breath, no doubt wishing I'd drop the subject altogether, grabbing a fan adorned with our father's face from the back pocket of the pew in front of us and fanning herself.

"Well, I was." I returned. "And I think—"

"Stop it!" She yelled, voice blending with the choir as the altos and sopranos all joined in on the chorus, forcing over half the congregation to their feet clapping and shouting and the whole nine.

"Cool." I shook my head. I knew when my sister'd had enough. Her eyes were glistening, and her lip was trembling. I rubbed her shoulder to show sincerity. "I'm sorry."

She nodded and exhaled as I gripped her hand. Our family had more issues than seasons one through six of Dr. Phil. But this one, in particular, was overdue for resolve.

"Good morning, Tabernacle!" My father's voice came blaring through the sound system in perfect timing as the choir took their seats after a stellar performance.

Penny's eyes lit up with relief and admiration. She turned into a little girl every time our father entered the sanctuary on Sunday without fail.

"This is the day that the Lord has made…" My father stated just as he had for nearly sixteen hundred Sundays.

"We shall rejoice and be glad in it." The entire congregation said in unison.

"Amen," Pops said. "If you don't mind, I'm gonna ask that you remain standing for a moment." He made his way down the aisle from the back of the church and up to the pulpit, taking his place behind the podium.

"Tabernacle, I got some good news and I got some bad news

this morning." He spoke somberly, sending a ripple of *oh no's* traveling from the front pew to the back.

"Yeah, we got a, umm, a dilemma of sorts." He squinted, running his tongue under his top lip the way he always did right before he was about to crack a joke.

The congregation might not've caught that hint, but I'd committed my father's mannerisms to memory. It'd saved me from many ass whippings deciphering what he *said* from what he *meant*.

"Now I know that many of you came here for the word of God. *Amen?*" He nodded and most of the congregation Amen'd in agreement.

"But there are a few that I won't judge who come for the mouthwatering Tabernacle Brunch. Somebody stop me when I start lyin'." He widened his eyes and a mixture of laughter and gasps spread throughout the church.

"Amen. It's alright." He huffed. "The good news is that for those of you who came for the Word, we got plenty." He nodded, panning the audience.

"But the bad news, Amen." He paused to inhale the way most pastors do for reasons that common folk wouldn't and couldn't understand. "The bad news is that if you came through those twelve-foot wooden doors for brunch on this morning, we're a few croissant sandwiches short due to the absence of Sister Opal."

"Awwe man!" A visitor a few pews back shouted pulling every single eye in his direction.

Brave as hell.

"Don't worry brother, Sister Opal's ok," Pops mentioned, knowing full well that brother with his belly sitting four inches down his lap, wasn't concerned with Sister Opal's well-being. "She's away on a cruise. Even the blessed hands of the Brunch Ministry need a vacation. Amen?"

"Amen!" Sister Liles, an ex-member of the Brunch Ministry, shouted in agreement from the second, center pew, garnering several eye rolls from the congregation because everybody knew she got voted out for putting too much salt in the scrambled eggs.

And I have no doubt in my mind that if Pops would've spoken the bad news about brunch a little bit louder, sisters Rose and Lilly would've gotten up and left their seats. Luckily for him, they were hard of hearing. But there'd be hell to pay when they got back to the dining hall to find that the kitchen assistants were attempting to feed an entire congregation with one fish and a loaf of bread, and neither of them were Jesus.

"We'll make do." Pops nodded his head as the congregation whispered amongst themselves. "But you're welcome to leave without judgment if the Word ain't what you came for."

The end of that statement surprised me. And what surprised me, even more, was that a handful of people actually stood and raised a pointer finger as they headed toward the chapel doors. Pops didn't even look their way as he opened up his old worn Bible filled to the brim with post-it notes. Instead navigating his way to the words that would directly relate to the situation at hand. He wasn't new to this, he was true to this. There was always a lesson on the way.

"Looks like we got a few leavers. *Amen.*" He peeped up from the Good Book for a second signaling that he'd found what he called *The Fruit.*

The four or so people that had left their seats had now stopped in their tracks, a couple turning around, eyes darting from one pew to the next.

"But ain't it a good thing that God is not like man?" Pops asked, directing the question to every soul, both sitting and standing.

"Ain't it a blessing to know that he won't walk out on us when we don't give him what he asked for?" He continued, voice slightly changing pitch as he embarked on what would be this Sunday's subject matter.

"If God's been good to you this morning and gave you legs strong enough to remain standing, won't you follow me to where I'm about to go?"

It was amazing how he phrased a command and made it sound like a request. Those that knew him well enough stayed on their feet, Bibles in hand, ready to navigate their ways to the designated passage.

"Saints, come and go with me to Matthew six, verses twenty-five through twenty-six." He said with conviction.

I carefully slid Boogie from under my arm, laying her sleepy head on a pillow that Penny'd pulled from a bottomless backpack that housed everything but the kitchen sink. We stood, sharing a Bible that she'd been carrying for longer than she could read. And we read along with the Tabernacle as instructed by our father, Pastor Chadwick Fold Sr.

"25 Therefore I tell you, do not worry about your life, what you will eat or drink; or about your body, what you will wear. Is not life more than food, and the body more than clothes? 26 Look at the birds of the air; they do not sow or reap or store away in barns, and yet your heavenly Father feeds them. Are you not much more valuable than they?"

We all paused, looking to Pastor Fold for direction. And he gave it expeditiously, directing us to verses thirty-two and thirty-three in the same book.

It read:

"32 For the pagans run after all these things, and your heavenly Father knows that you need them. 33 But seek first his kingdom and his righteousness, and all these things will be given to you as well."

Removing his reading glasses and placing them beside the open Bible, he peered out into the crowd, seamlessly taking a deep breath that would propel him through the duration of his sermon.

"I don't know what you came in the Tabernacle for this morning." He said, eyes steady and sure and identical to my own.

"I don't know the desires of your heart, your wallet, or your stomach" He panned the audience, many of which were already shouting.

"But the Lord will provide. Even when you decide that what he already gave you is no longer sufficient, he'll still keep on providing. Do I have a witness?" He asked, already knowing that he was right.

"See, some folks came in here hungry." He stepped back from the podium, grabbing a neatly folded white handkerchief that had been laid to the left of his Bible by his longtime assistant, Sister Barbara Bimage.

"You, you, you walked through the church doors with your mind set on one thing, because you heard about it." He strategically stuttered through his statement. "Heard we got a brunch cooking up back there in that kitchen that'll make you slap yo' mama. And, Mama, I'm sorry, but it's the truth, Tabernacle!" He waved that handkerchief in the air like a staff from the Lord's hand, pointing up to my dear grandmother in Heaven who had passed away almost twenty years ago.

"I've eaten pancakes at IHOP and waffles at the Waffle House, and Lord knows I love me some fish and grits from The Breakfast Club. But don't none of 'em hold a candle to what the Brunch Ministries put together back through those doors." He pointed to a set of doors that led to the kitchen and dining area.

"So, trust me when I say that I understand why folks would be busting down the doors of the church to get in here for a bite. I know what it means to be hungry for something. I can testify to the desire to have a pancake that covers the whole plate, soaked in enough syrup to cover the floors of this church. But if God didn't say that I can have it—somebody better shut me up 'fore I go too far!" Pops stopped himself, did a hoop and a holler, pulling an entire row of sisters leaping in their kitten heels.

"If God didn't say I could have it, then Tabernacle, it ain't mine." He continued.

"I don't care how early you showed up for it. I don't care if you put on your sharpest suit or your prettiest dress. If God didn't say you could have that thing, that thing don't belong to you."

He pointed a long finger out into the congregation, directing that statement at nobody or everybody, depending on where they stood in life. You could feel the ripple of relatability traveling from one pew to the next. Spirits waking up and realizing that the word was for them and that the hand of God had placed them in the right seat on the right pew in the right church on that day.

"Now I'm not sayin' that the Lord don't want you to have brunch, Tabernacle." Pops wiped away the sweat beading on his forehead. "The Lord wants you to eat. Ecclesiastes nine and seven says *'Go, eat your food with gladness, and drink your wine with a joyful heart...'* It's your intentions he's concerned with." He said.

"An ill-willed heart can't carry the word of God, nor can it receive His blessings fully." His pause for a deep breath signaled scattered applause and a few agreement shouts.

"I'm not gon' keep you long." He'd caught his breath and told the truth. Many Pastors promised to keep it brief, but my father was one of the ten percent that actually kept their word.

"And I promise, we're gonna feed you 'cause I don't need nobody bad-mouthing the Tabernacle on *Three Peas Morning Show*. Amen?" A group of youngsters sitting in the row across from ours had to cover their mouths, sitting in disbelief that the pastor even knew what *Three Peas* was although his youngest daughter cohosted the show.

"But before you nourish your body with refreshments that our Brunch Ministry has prepared for you," He gently laid his handkerchief down on the podium before looking up and out into the audience.

"Understand that there is an alternate form of nourishment that you should be seeking when you walk through those two wooden doors." He whooped with the pianist keying up to add a melodic backdrop where my father's words fell.

"Bear in mind, Tabernacle, that there is a tray of goodness prepared by our Father in Heaven for us to eat from each and every day." He shouted, stepping from behind the podium.

"Let the record show that there is not a block of cheese sliced forty different ways that can compare to the word of the Father himself. And lest ye be filled by the power of his Holy name, ain't nothin' I can feed you that'll fill you up anyway. Can anybody hear me out there?"

Several shouts of praise sprung free from the lungs of those who got where Pops was going. I found myself clapping along with my sister, keyed in on his words like the lyrics to a song I'd heard before but needed to hear again.

"Anybody out there hungry for the word of God?" Pops asked, responses of praise pouring in like rain.

"Anybody out there been void of nourishment that couldn't be found on a dinner plate?" He slowly made his way down the set of steps leading from the stage to the foot of the altar.

"Anybody know how it feels to stand in the need of the bread of the Lord? *My God!"* He shouted, both hands raised as he waved them like the wings of an eagle.

"Come eat." His voice lowered to a near whisper. "Bring it all to the altar and be fed by the Lord. He will supply all of your needs. Even if you didn't come in here knowing what you needed from Him, God's got you."

My father's hands remained raised as a third of the congregation flocked to the altar, including the four people who'd almost left when they found out that brunch might be skimpy. Jada stood and brought the choir to their feet, singing a soft selection appropriate for *Altar Call* as weeping and the speaking of tongues swept the front of the church in the most beautiful kind of way.

I can't explain how this experience never failed to take my breath away. With my eyes closed, I could feel the presence of the Lord as if he were a physical being standing right beside me. My hands remained raised, numbness trickling down from the tips of my fingers to the points of my elbows rendering me nearly defenseless to the energies circling in this spirit-filled room. I was seconds away from being consumed by it all, left bare and exposed to the elements of the Holy Spirit. Then I remembered I wasn't alone and slowly dropped my arms. I hadn't been moved this far, this fast in a long, long time.

And it scared me.

Had me questioning why.

Penny gripped my hand, somehow knowing, even with her eyes closed, that I was into it, and standing in desperate need of something I didn't know how to ask for. Life was good, great even. But there were voids that needed filling. I'd been raised by a man of God and a woman whose intuition was like something from a sci-fi movie. And for those reasons alone, there was no way I could continue to ignore the calling on my life. Yet there I stood with the stench of a stranger's perfume still staining my nose hairs, almost completely filled with the Holy Spirit, unable to make available that small space where all the answers lie.

"I gotta go to the restroom." I leaned to the side and whispered in Penny's ear. My own thoughts were tugging at me too heavy to stand there and risk breaking down in front of all those people.

"You okay?" She looked up the slope of my arm and asked. *"I can come wipe your butt."*

"I'm good, man!" I smiled, planting a kiss on her cheek and raising a finger to exit the sanctuary.

Two

"I don't know if y'all are aware of the enormity of what's going, but in case I haven't made it crystal clear in the last sixty rehearsals, it's pretty fucking humongous to be going on tour with *the* Kenny "Plus" Washington. And you're not about to have me out here looking stupid with these subpar ass performances. So, for the three hundredth time, we're gonna take it from the top. Tootie and Fruity, step over here for a sec. I need to curse you out in private."

If the goal was to make us feel like incompetent pieces of shit, Kenny had hired the perfect person for the job. After thirty straight days of getting acquainted with complicated choreography, world-renowned dance coach, Jennifer Telfer, was no closer to being pleased with *The Crew* than she had been on the first day. She didn't give a damn that of the five of us, I was the only one who had ever received professional training, or that half of us didn't think dancing would be necessary in our genre. All she knew was that Kenny had hired her to transform us from kids who somewhat knew our way around the mic, to superstars who commanded the crowd's attention from the time we hit the stage until the second that we walked off.

Since Jennifer had traded in our actual names for *Tootie and Fruity*, Jock and I hurried over to the corner as ordered. Our bandmates, Bre, Sabre, and Kimi, fought the urge to laugh out loud while they took a quick break during me and Jock's tongue lashing.

"Taya, I know how much you hate the title, but you're the face of this group. The brand ambassador, if you will." Jennifer stated for what had to be the millionth time. "You're picking up the choreography better than the rest, but you're lacking leadership and that's not gonna cut it."

"But I didn't ask to be—"

"Nor did I *ask* for a rebuttal." She cut me off.

She was *always* cutting me off.

"And Jock." She took a deep breath then blew it out, sliding her eyes from me to the handsome butter-colored brother who'd been thrown into my path under the most mind-blowing circumstances. "I'm sure your ego leads you to believe that you're over here for the same reason as Taya. But you're not. Quite the opposite, actually. I have never seen a man with less rhythm in my life. It's like you're not even hearing the same track as everyone else. Do you honestly believe that anyone in their right mind would pay five dollars, let alone one hundred, to see you on that stage flailing around like a fish out of water? I mean look at you. You're the epitome of sexy, yet you dance like you don't know it. And in case I'm not getting my point across with all these little words, Sabre is making an ass out of you, scoring at least twenty points per rehearsal for the dark-skinned brothers. And don't tell me that's not still a thing."

It was amazing that so many words could come from the mouth of such a small woman. I was an even five eight and she stood at least three inches shorter than me. But her energy and the wind it must've taken to get through paragraph-long rants could easily increase her stature by three feet.

"No disrespect, Miss Jennifer, but I didn't sign up for all this dance shit." Jock's chocolate brown eyes never connected with Jennifer's because he wasn't the type to look into people's eyes unless he thought he could get something out of them. And he was smart enough to know that he wasn't getting anything out of Jennifer but a hard time.

"You didn't... I'm sorry, did you just say you didn't sign up for this?" Jennifer stepped closer to Jock, so close that if her breasts weren't so flat, they might have pressed into his stomach.

"By a show of hands, how many of you signed up for this... what did you call it, Jock?" She looked up at him and asked, then waited for his response because that's the kind of thing she did.

"Dance... shit." Jock nearly whispered, hating the fact that she was putting him on the spot.

"I'm sorry, we didn't hear you. Did y'all hear him?" She turned to the rest of *The Crew* whose faces were tight from trying not to laugh.

"No." Bre was the first to respond, making it more apparent that she couldn't stand Jock.

Sabre and Kimi kept it calm and didn't say anything, not that it was necessary for Jennifer to take it further.

"I said, I didn't sign up for this dance shit. Or this public humiliation shit either." Jock let loose. "And if Plus wanted to cast a damn Chris Brown video, he shoulda said that."

"And if he had, where would you be?" Jennifer folded her arms across her chest, thigh muscles visible through her silver tights, mahogany skin smooth and bold to match the tone of her voice.

Jock decided against responding to the question because we all knew where he'd be and it sure as hell wasn't opening for one of the greatest emcees to grace the stage.

"That's what I thought." Jennifer uncrossed her arms, clapping her hands together to signal us back into place on the rehearsal floor. Everyone else rushed to their marked spots as Jennifer's assistant prepared to start the record. But Jock was too flustered to focus, I guess, exiting the room and letting the door slam behind him.

"Jennifer, can I—"

"Please do." She dismissed me before I could finish my request.

I grabbed my towel from a bench beside the exit door, looking back to find Bre standing there shaking her head. I knew Jock wasn't a baby. Hell, everybody did. But he didn't have family to call on when he was having a bad day. I'd been that for him since we started Plus Academy.

"You okay?" I found him crouched down by the restroom door, as usual, head down, eyes on his phone, searching for things he never wanted me to see.

"I'm good. She send you out here?" He killed the phone screen and dragged his eyes up to me. Eyes that held more pain than he'd ever share with a counselor although I'd begged him to do so a thousand times.

"No." I eased down onto the floor beside him. "She never sends me out here. But she also never tells me no when I ask to come. She's not the devil, Jock."

"Nah. She's his sister." He shook his head, a bead of sweat sliding down the side of his face. "You think Plus knows she's goin' hard on us like that? Some of this shit don't seem necessary."

I used my towel to wipe the sweat off his face and said, "I don't think he knows. I *know* he knows. He hired the best because that's what he wants us to be. And you don't get to that level by walking out of rehearsals every time it gets too hard."

"Oh really?"

"Yes *really*." I offered a smile because it felt like he needed one.

"Yeah, that would be your response, since you're perfect and shit." He didn't seem receptive of my friendly spirit. But instead of taking it personally, I chalked it up to him being in a bad mood.

"I'm not perfect." I folded the towel up and stood up from the floor, extending a hand to help him up too. "But I'm not gonna get any closer to it by sitting out here moping and neither are you. So, let's go."

"Nah," He refused my hand and stood up on his own. "Actually, I think I'mma head out."

He took a swig from the water bottle he'd been holding and started to back away toward the exit door.

"Tell JT I'll see her tomorrow!" He yelled from the door, water bottle echoing off the lobby walls as it crashed into the bottom of the trash can.

Three

Music from a record we were collaborating on blared through the Bluetooth speaker mounted on the counter of my vanity table as my bandmate and friend, Bre, carefully installed a set of unnecessarily long lashes over her moon-shaped eyes. Me, her and my childhood friend, Kanika, were stepping out for the night. And as tired as I was, I was overjoyed to see more than the rehearsal room since Jennifer had finally given us a break after running us ragged for a month straight.

My high-waist jeans and long-sleeved, yellow cropped sweater paled in comparison to the neon purple skin-tight bodysuit covering Bre's voluptuous figure from neck to toe. It wouldn't be Bre if she didn't take it over the top. This girl never left the house without looking like the signature piece at an art exhibit. Kanika, on the other hand, fell somewhere in between. Choosing a flowy pant romper that camouflaged the trouble spots that I'm convinced she was imagining. The girl was as slim as a toothpick, living off of maybe two salads a day.

"I don't know how you see anything with those bat wings on your eyes." Kanika took a jab at Bre. The two had been like oil and water since I introduced them three months prior. I don't know what their beef was about, but I wished they'd squash it already.

"The same way I'm about to strut past hating bitches like you in the club; with confidence." Bre looked over her shoulder at Kanika, dragging her eyes up and down her lanky frame and rolling them back to the mirror when she was finished.

"Am I gonna have to hear this all night?" I stood beside Bre in the mirror, applying edge control to my edges. "If I wanted to be stressed out by other people's voices I coulda went to the studio and waited for Jennifer to show up."

"She's just jealous," Bre smirked, sucking her teeth.

"Of what, too much ass and not enough class?" Kanika returned, taking a seat in one of the chairs beside my bed and flipping out her phone.

"Girl, fuck you." Bre shot the finger at Kanika.

"With that deep ass voice, I wouldn't be surprised if you pulled out a dick." Kanika rolled her levered eyes.

"Trust me, if I had one, you wouldn't be worthy." Bre chuckled.

"Seriously!?" I cut in. "Just one night. *One* damn night. That's all I'm asking." I reached in my jewelry box and picked out a pair of golden hooped earrings that my mama'd bought me for my birthday.

"Fine. But I'm not the problem." Bre replied, lashes almost kissing her forehead as she blinked her eyes open and stared into the vanity mirror in my restroom.

"Whatever. Is Jock gonna be there?" Kanika asked out of nowhere. I don't know why she was always inquiring about my ex. I got that she was a fan but the shit was becoming annoying.

"I don't know. Probably." I replied while putting on my earrings.

"I hope so. I promised Nel an autograph and a selfie."

"Girl, you'd be lucky to get Jock to spit on you let alone sign something for your little sister, wearing that too big ass romper."

Bre was taking harsh to a new level. She knew Kanika had body issues.

I made a mental note to never entertain them at the same time again.

"You might find it hard to believe, but not everybody wants to look like a Kardashian," Kanika said, sitting back in her chair.

"Girl, the *Kardashians* don't even look like Kardashians." Bre spat out a giggle. "Them bitches tryna look like me."

"You wish." Kanika rolled her eyes.

"You know what *I* wish? I wish you both would shut the fuck up." I sighed, rolling my eyes as I sat on the edge of the bathtub, sliding my feet into a pair of golden four-inch Louboutin's and securing the strap around my ankles.

Bre caught my reflection in the mirror and asked, "You good?"

"Yeah, I'm good. I'm just tired. And you should be too after surviving JT's boot camp. Kanika's only down for a few days and it would be nice if y'all could get along. You're both my girls. But when you're together you make it hard to remember why I like either one of you." I got up from the bathtub and stood beside Bre in the mirror, heels sitting my behind at attention as I pulled a headful of waist-length braids over my shoulder.

"Girl, stop playin'." Bre tapped a blush brush in my direction with the tip of her long fingernail. "You and I both know you love me 'cause I'm the realest bitch you ever met." She pursed her full, glossed lips.

"I'm literally dying to see how real you are underneath those bundles and lashes." Kanika killed her phone screen, probably ending a google search on some keto diet that she didn't need to go on.

"Why don't you just literally *die*?" Bre snapped. The girl's mouth was reckless.

"Stop." I blew out a breath. "And that's the last time I'm saying it."

"Or what?" Kanika had the nerve to ask.

"*Or what?*" Bre spoke before I could. "Bitch you ain't paid for nothin' since you got here. You might wanna mind before you get put on a Greyhound and sent back to Waxahachie."

"I am *not* from Waxahachie." Kanika defended.

"Waxahachie, Huntsville. Same damn thing." Bre taunted as I headed for the door replying to a text from security.

"Wait, where you goin'?" Bre noticed and asked.

"To wait in the car for whichever one of you survives this stupid catfight." I looked back over my shoulder as they hurried to gather their things, then let the door swing behind me until they raced to get out of it first.

"Wait, she's how old?"

Anybody who knew Sabre knew that he didn't want it if it didn't have gray hair on it. So, I was surprised as hell when he told me that some chick he was meeting at Bottom's was less than forty-five years old.

"Nigga, you heard me. Twenty-two." He elbowed me, panning the crowd for the one-hundredth time as we sat in a booth in the far corner of the club, chopping it up and watching the crowd filter in.

It had only been a few weeks since the last time we hit up Bottoms and I was praying to God I didn't run into old girl from the bachelor party. If Sabre hadn't guilted me into coming back tonight before *The Crew* went on tour, I would've been happily lying in my bed being boring as usual.

"Look, there they go." Sabre pointed across the crowded dance floor. Our booth was elevated so we had the perfect view. It didn't take me a split second to see exactly who he was talking about.

Two huge security guards ushered in three beautiful women, one wearing a one-piece outfit that looked like it had been painted on, another being swallowed up by a flowy romper, and the other bringing life to a pair of high-waist skinny jeans and cropped sweater that would've looked boring as hell on anybody else. The volume of the crowd multiplied by one hundred and the DJ validated the identity of two of the beauties by shouting their names on the mic.

"Alright, H-town. We got some royalty in the building!" He screamed. *"Welcome to Bottoms, Bre, and Taya Maxey. We see y'all!"* He scratched the record and put on the latest record from The Crew, *"New Money"*.

Cameras flashed and screams grew louder as Taya and Bre posed for pics and the third chick fell to the side, painting on a fake smile with security keeping a tight watch. Within a few minutes, they'd made it over to where me and Sabre were sitting, seemingly out of breath after pushing through the crowd. The collar of my T-shirt tightened around my neck. This was the second time I'd seen Taya in person and her presence definitely brought back that same exact static.

"Wassup, Sabe?" Bre spoke first. And I could not get over how tall she was. Me and Sabre stood about six-two apiece, and she was damn near looking my boy in the eyes.

"Wassup Bre'elle?" Sabre had a habit of calling people by their government names. Did the shit to me all the time and I could tell Bre was annoyed.

"You ain't gon' be happy until I stab your black ass." She shoved a long, sharp fingernail into his chest before he pulled her into a friendly hug and stepped aside as her eyes slid to me.

"And you are?" She asked while Taya and Sabre exchanged hugs and greetings with the romper chick standing by looking hella uncomfortable.

"Chad. Nice to meet you...again" I extended for a handshake.

"Ooooh, Selfie Nigga!" She put a hand to her mouth,

completely over-exaggerating. "The PK who had the whole world thinking my girl Taya was converting to Christianity. I didn't think we'd see you again."

Before I knew it, I'd been pulled into a tight hug that lasted long enough to feel welcoming, but not long enough to feel flirtatious. Bre was a stallion, no doubt. Brick house down to the bone. It was no wonder she'd made it into Plus Academy. She was repping for the cornbread fed.

"I'on't know about all that. But yeah, that's me." I grinned, but Taya did not.

"Converted from what, Bre?" Taya smirked at her friend.

"I don't know. Heathenism, maybe?" Bre was a character.

Taya simply rolled her eyes and landed them on me again. "Hey, Chad." She said with trace amounts of enthusiasm.

"Wassup?" I nodded. And neither of us offered a handshake, hug, or stick of gum.

"You tell me." She stepped in and took a seat. And I had no idea what that was supposed to mean.

Sabre, Bre, and the third chick, Kanika, sat down after me, with Sabre and Bre falling into conversation the way siblings do at family gatherings, almost completely ignoring Kanika who was apparently the date Sabre had mentioned earlier. I could tell from their body language that neither of them found each other attractive. But Sabre was too much of a gentleman to say that to the girl's face. I felt bad just witnessing the awkwardness of it all. There was way more chemistry between Sabre and Bre.

I leaned forward and checked a few notifications on my phone, pretending Taya didn't exist because it was easier than staring at her trying to figure out the color of her eyes. Somewhere between copper, brown and cinnamon from what I'd gathered at a glance. It was the type of thing you could get lost in if you weren't careful.

"So, how've you been?" She didn't seem nearly as bubbly as she'd been the time before. She was still pretty, of course. But her flicker was dim.

"Good." I coolly looked up from my phone. Keeping my cool around her was like exercising a muscle I'd never used. *"You?"* I hiked a brow, taking her in on a sigh.

"I've been good." She breathed out. "Just tired, you know? Rehearsals and interviews, and—"

"You know what, can you excuse me for a minute?" I was trying my damndest to concentrate on her words. But the urge to take her hand and put it to my chest so she could feel how hard my heart was beating was so strong.

"Yeah, sure." She must've been shocked. I doubt anybody with eyes, ears, or good sense would leave her presence voluntarily.

"Damn, y'all couldn't let a nigga know where y'all was postin' up?" Just before I stood up, a light-skinned cat that I recognized as Jock, entered our section with a bottle in hand and a fat gold chain hanging around his neck that looked like it weighed a hundred pounds. Rumor had it him and Taya were on for a minute, but she dropped him for reasons that I didn't have the time nor desire to research.

"Lord, here go *this* nigga." Bre sucked her teeth and rolled her eyes. Jock had stepped right in front of Taya and looked down at me.

"Could you move, please?" Taya looked up into Jock's eyes. The brother looked loaded and I was hoping he didn't cause a scene.

"Why? You too good to sit with me now?" Jock slurred, a trickle of spit from his mouth accidentally falling on Taya's cheek.

"Jock, come on man." Sabre slid forward in his seat as Taya wiped Jock's spit off her face.

"Man, shut up." Jock looked back and threw a hand at Sabre dismissively. "Act like y'all fuckin' or somethin'. You fuckin' Sabe now, Tay?" A sinister chuckle rolled from his mouth.

"Say, man, chill with all that." I stood up, not at all in the mood for watching this dude act a fool.

"*What?* Nigga, who the fuck is you?" Jock smirked at me,

putting his bottle down on the table and taking a step back away from Taya.

"Jock, stop." Taya tried grabbing his hand. He yanked away and almost slapped her in the process.

"Are you serious?" Now Bre was up and looked ready to fight.

"Cha Cha, we headin' out." Sabre stood up behind Jock and alerted the security guard that had made her way into the booth while Jock stared me in the face. "Chad, let's go." Sabre nodded, raising his voice, snapping me out of a heated stare down that would've likely ended with me cracking his boy's jaw.

"Nah, let the nigga say what he gotta say." Jock dragged. "Looks like lame niggas roll together 'round this bitch."

"The only thing lame is that unnecessary ass chain around your neck." Bre bucked, running a finger under the back of Jock's chain after she'd pushed past him, grabbing ahold of Taya's hand.

And then, before either of us saw it coming, Jock turned around and cocked his arm back, just inches away from punching Bre in the face when I grabbed his arm and Sabre grabbed the other. Security grabbed what was left of his body, snatching him from me and Sabre and dragging him out of the section all the way to the front door. I straightened my clothes and made sure the ladies were okay, then I headed for the door myself.

"Man, what the fuck was that?" Sabre hurried alongside me as Cha Cha escorted us and the ladies out of the club. Things had escalated so quickly, I didn't have a chance to catch my breath and Taya kept looking back at me as she was being rushed through the crowd, eyes filled with questions that I probably couldn't answer.

"What you mean?" I tried hard not to make eye contact with Taya as we neared the exit. "You were right there. That nigga's crazy."

"Nah, not Jock," Sabre said dismissively. "He's always on some bullshit. I'm talking about you and Taya."

"What about us?"

"Chad, you know damn well what I'm talkin' about. I thought you moved past that, bro."

"And I did." I looked to the side at him as we moved through the crowd. "At least I'm trying to. She ain't into voodoo or nothin' is she?"

"What? Nah. Why you say that?" Sabre chuckled.

"Nothin. It's... nothin'."

"It's the Tay effect." Bre offered, popping up beside us. "I'mma check on her. And thanks for putting on your cape. Sabre only puts *his* on one shoulder." She rolled her eyes at my boy and hurried off on a set of heels so high, an amateur would've broken both ankles.

"Umm, I'm gonna go too." Kanika appeared like a phantom, almost running into the back of Bre. And as skinny as she was, that would've been unfortunate. She woulda disappeared into the crack of Bre's ass.

"Bro, I told you to leave that alone." Sabre shook his head after the ladies had left. "You're gonna mess around and get yourself killed comin' at Taya like that."

"*Killed*? What, y'all Illuminati?" I huffed.

"Nah, it's just… she ain't like that." He said. "And Plus might not appreciate your tactics. That's basically his daughter now."

"Y'all act like Plus is out here murdering niggas. And aside from that, I'm not comin' at her sideways. I'm not comin' at her at all."

"Chad, that don't even make sense." Sabre laughed, looking up as security helped Bre and Kanika into the Jeep where Taya was already seated. "I ain't never seen you sit next to a woman without doin' what you do."

"And what is that?" I pretended not to know. Granted, I had my ways, I was innocent this time.

"Look, people change." I defended when Sabre declined to answer my question.

"Yeah, but you ain't *people*." He tipped his chin.

"You make it sound like I'm a monster."

"Cause you *are*." He hiked a brow, stopping just outside the doors of the club, unfazed by all the people screaming his name when they realized who he was. "And that's cool. One of us has to maintain the player status."

"Nigga, please. Just because you be shopping for pussy in nursing homes doesn't mean you're exempt from being labeled a sleaze."

"A sleaze?"

"A sleaze!"

"Man, go to hell." He dismissed me with a waved hand, cameras flashing all over the place, screams so loud we had to yell through the rest of the conversation.

"I can't." I shrugged. "PK pass on lock." I traced a hand up and down and across my chest and kissed it up to God.

"Yeah, you really goin' now." Sabre busted out laughing, and I had no choice but to do the same.

"Real talk though, what's up with you and Bre?" I wouldn't be a friend if I didn't ask.

"Shit." His response was too quick for my liking. "Bre's like a sister. Gotta keep business and pleasure separate."

"Sister my ass. You had a whole woman sitting between y'all and she might as well have been invisible."

"Who, Ericka?" He squinted.

"Her name's Kanika, which proves my point." I chuckled.

"Listen, you're worried about the wrong thing." He elbowed the side of my arm. "That's what's wrong with your ass now. Don't make me hit the prayer line and tell Pastor Fold you need to be re-baptized."

I howled because this man was dead serious. Back in high

school, he literally called the Tabernacle Prayer Line and had the whole congregation lifting me in prayer for the demons encouraging my heathen spirit. I was on punishment for the duration of the football season that year and the only company I could have over was Sabre since he'd assisted in "saving my soul". The prank worked so well he threatened me with it anytime I didn't go along with his shenanigans. And apparently, my boy was still childish as hell.

"You stupid." I shook my head, suddenly reminded that my bladder was full. "I'mma head out." I tipped my chin, taking a quick glance toward the hummer and catching Taya's eyes on me from the back seat.

"You sure you don't wanna roll?" Sabre offered. "We'll probably hit the studio and make a diss track to tease Jock with once he sobers up."

"Nah, I'm good," I replied. "And honestly, I'm not amused by this shit. Y'all should probably tell your boy to get some counseling before he bucks up to the wrong one."

"Oh, so you a Menace to Society now? I see you O-Dog!" He clapped my shoulder and I laughed though I was far from playing. Taya wasn't mine to protect or stand up for but seeing that fool come at her like that sent me straight into action.

"You know that ain't me." I shook my head, pulling my cell from my back pocket to check an incoming text.

"Exactly. Which makes it even more obvious that you have a thing for Taya and even more important that you understand the words that are coming out of my mouth."

"Go 'head." I sighed. Sabre was more of a preacher than my pops sometimes.

"Either come at her right or fall back." He simply stated.

"Aight, Sabe." I extended for a handshake.

He gripped my palm and said, "I'm serious, bro. I would hate to see your face on one of those missing person's posts on Facebook behind some bullshit."

"Bro, I heard you the first, second, and third time." I chuckled.

"And I'm good on all that. Seriously. She ain't even my type."

"Maaaaan bye!" He dragged, turning away from me and heading off to the Hummer. "Lyin' ass nigga!" He yelled without looking back and all I could do was laugh.

I struggled to grasp what was going on. Feeling things that didn't make sense for a man I barely knew. His demeanor had changed, granted, mine had too since I lacked the liquid courage I possessed the last time we spoke due to Jennifer putting us on a strict, non-alcoholic diet. Maybe that was the reason he couldn't look me in the face either. I didn't smell anything on his breath except Spearmint gum.

Be that as it may, there was still something there. Memories of his arms around my waist, the scent of his cologne lingering on my blouse the next day. It all came rushing back the minute he sat beside me in that booth. I thought I'd moved past it, but apparently, I hadn't.

"You sure you don't wanna roll?" Sabre asked as Chad stood near the door of the club checking something on his cell.

"Nah, I'm good." He looked up. "Think I've had enough action for the night." His eyes slid to me and I damn near melted in my seat.

He bowed his head and started to walk away, hands tucked in the pockets of a pair of jeans that hung off his statuesque frame, teetering a thin line between street and saved. Every fiber of my being wanted to jump out and run behind him. To thank him for showing concern when he didn't really have to. But I doubted he'd be receptive. He only stood up to Jock because it was the Christian thing to do. He was the perfect blend of sinner and saved, the kind of man who should be avoided at all costs.

But, "Cha Cha wait!" I disregarded common sense, reaching

out and tapping the arm of my security guard, a tall, thick sister who didn't fear anything but mice and bees. "I'm going with him." I slid to the end of the seat and climbed out, feeling Chad's eyes on me as soon as my heels hit the pavement.

Cha Cha tipped her chin up at Mo, the head of security who'd be driving the vehicle I'd just climbed out of, letting him know that she was gonna roll out with me.

"I don't need you, Cha Cha." I looked back over my shoulder. "He got me." I returned my eyes to the coffee brown brother standing less than five feet away.

"You do have me, right?" I hiked a brow, extending my hand like we'd been doing this for years instead of ten damn minutes.

He threw his head back and slid his eyes from me to Cha Cha, giving the impression that he did, in fact, have me. And then he said, "I don't think that's a good idea." And shitted on my ego as he turned back around and continued on down the pavement.

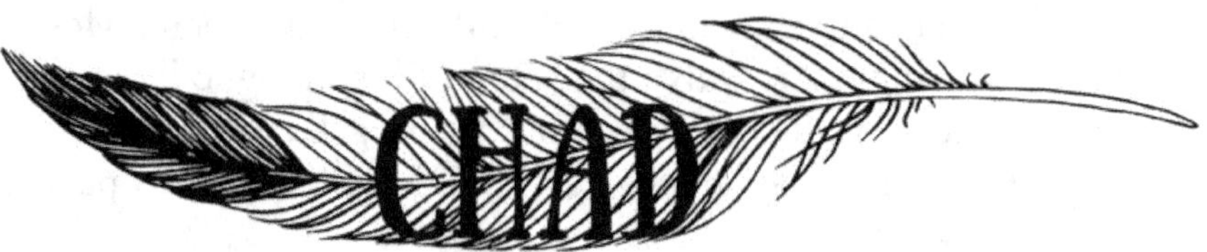

I wanted to call her, but I felt stupid.

I wanted to apologize but didn't know what I was sorry for.

I wanted to grab her hand when she asked if I had her, but it didn't feel like the right thing to do.

I wanted this whole situation to be easier than it was, but apparently, that wasn't gonna be the case.

Typically, when faced with a problem that I couldn't take care of on my own, I'd pray about it and wait for God to reveal the answer. But this wasn't some business endeavor or a new client who wanted a tattoo of Jesus on their butt cheek. This was a girl. No, a *woman* that had me thinking too much beyond our initial encounter. This hadn't happened to me since the first grade when Melody Printess gave me my first kiss in exchange for a cherry tootsie pop, and the price of kisses had gone up exponentially since then, especially when you wanted one from someone you probably shouldn't even be interested in.

Having decided that God alone couldn't help me with this situation, I fell back against my pillow after washing the night's stress away in the shower and called up the only person who might know what to say.

"Jay, you busy?" She'd picked up on the second ring, so I knew the answer to that question.

"If I was busy, I wouldn't be listening to you ask me that stupid question right now. What do you want?" My sister asked with an attitude. I'd probably interrupted her getting ready for church the next morning.

"Why you gotta be so rude?" I complained, flipping on the TV for background noise before I talked myself out of asking the question at hand. "I need to ask you something."

"Chad, would you just spit it out?" She fussed. "Drew's hitting me up for a phone boning session in like thirty minutes and I can't miss that."

"You know what." I almost threw up in my mouth. "You and Penny goin' straight to hell for the shit y'all be puttin' me through."

She laughed hard in my ear, settling down and encouraging me to go on with my problem once she'd gotten it all out of her system.

I started, "It's about a woman."

"Figured. I'm on my way."

"No. Not one I'm tryna get rid of." I calmed my sister down before she came over with a fake emergency to save me from a chick who wasn't getting the *get the fuck out my house* hint.

"Wait. You… you're not falling in lo—"

"I'm not in a position to be using that word right now, sis." I stopped her in her tracks. "But I'm *in like*…I think. Actually, I think I'm being hypnotized. Are Christians even susceptible to that kinda shit?" I'd confused myself but expected her to not be confused.

"Ok, so, I'm gonna go with *I don't know*. As in *I don't know what the hell you just said*." Jada chose sarcasm when I was serious as hell. But I got it. I didn't know what I'd said either.

"Look, if I tell you who it is it'll make more sense. But you can't tell nobody. Swear you won't tell nobody."

"I won't." She returned too quick. I needed to put a healthy threat on the table.

"Jada, if you tell anybody what I'm about to tell you I'm tellin' Pops you smashed Drew in his study that time y'all both came down for Christmas your Junior year at PLU."

"What? How did you—"

"Penny!" We both said at the same time.

"I swear she's a hater." Jada fumed. "Fine, you asshole. And this better be good. You got five minutes."

"I thought you said Drew was calling in thirty." I reminded her.

"Yes. But that was five minutes ago, and I need ten minutes to get my supplies together. You know, lube, whips, handcuffs, anal bea—"

"Stop, man!" I pulled the phone from my ear and wiped the screen. "Just stop."

She busted out laughing. "Fine. Go ahead, lil ugly boy."

I took a deep breath as if saying Taya's name might melt me just as quickly as seeing her face had. The thought of leaving her there on the sidewalk made me feel like shit, and it had been all I could do not to turn around and apologize.

But I couldn't.

The damage had already been done.

"It's Taya." I disclosed before I wound up talking myself out of it.

"Taya who?" Jada squeaked. "And please tell me it's not that bipolar girl who keyed my car thinking it was yours."

"What? No. That was *Laya*. Speaking of which, I need to make sure that restraining order is still active."

"Please do." Jada agreed. "Anyway, I still don't know who you're talking about. Wait, you don't mean... *Taya Maxey*? Chad..."

"I know. I know, you think I'm being stupid."

"If you're thinking about pursuing her, hell yeah, you're being stupid."

"But why though?" I sat straight up in my bed. I needed to give this conversation my undivided attention. "Am I really that bad?"

"Brother, have you met yourself?" Jada's voice was laced with judgment. "I mean I love you but—"

"I like her, Jay." I cut her off. "And it would be easier to say that I don't know why. But I do."

"I'm dying to hear this. Also, you got three minutes." I could hear her wrists popping to look at a watch that wasn't there.

"It's the *feather effect*."

"You're shittin' me right?"

"I wish I was," I replied. "I've seen her twice and it's been the same feeling both times. I can't even look at her too long without having to look away."

The *feather effect* was something my mother had told me would hit me sooner or later, signaling the end of the sewing of my wild oats. She said when the right one came along, it would be as subtle as a feather falling on my shoulder. Only the feather would never float away.

"Have you told her?" The tone in Jada's voice told me that she'd literally leaned into the conversation.

"Hell no!" I blurted. "I can't have her thinking I'm crazy."

"Hmm..." Jada teased.

"I'm not crazy." I defended.

"Really? Then what do you call it?"

"I call it… Shit, I don't know what to call it. But I'm not crazy."

A brief pause indicated that Jada was probably shooting a text to Jet and that kind of grossed me out, so I broke the silence and said "I don't know what I'm supposed to do. This ain't exactly familiar territory, and I think I might've messed up already."

"What? When? Y'all have been around each other a total of four damn hours. And speaking of time, you have two minutes." She was really clocking me.

Damn freak.

"Tonight, at Bottoms. After Bottoms, actually. She kind of invited herself to roll with me after some shit blew up, and I turned her down."

"Turned her down, why?"

"Cause I was scared."

"Chad, you got exactly forty-five seconds to tell me who you are and what you did with my brother. You haven't been scared of girls since you got that kiss from slutty Mel in the first grade."

"She was seven."

"She kissed you for candy." I could tell she was serious. Trifling as hell and serious. "That's grounds for early admission into Hoe-Ville. Fifteen seconds. The clock is ticking."

"I haven't thought about smashing her yet. I'm over here daydreaming about hugs and kisses and shit."

Jada remained silent while I waited for a response.

"Say something." I finally spoke.

"When you say kisses…"

"On the lips, Jay. And you know I don't kiss nobody's lips."

"Damn." She sounded legitimately surprised. And rightfully so because kisses lingered long after they were placed and that's the reason I didn't kiss women. To avoid misinterpretations of what they thought we could be.

"All I have to say is that either you're coming down with something or aliens really do exist. Either way, I gotta get off this phone."

"Jay!"

"Love you, bye!" She yelled into the phone before ending the call and our conversation without being any help at all.

The logical next step was to call my mother about the *feather effect* kicking in, but our conversations hadn't lasted for more than three minutes for the last two years. We were in an awkward place; our whole family was, really. And as bad as I needed to bounce this situation off her ears, I wasn't ready to open up that door.

Not yet.

Four

The First Semester Tour with Plus would be kicking off in a matter of days. Our promotion team had been killing it on social media, resulting in sold-out shows from Houston to New York City. *The Crew* was hype, myself included, despite the drama going on between me and Jock, and the embarrassment of literally being left hanging by Chad. All our dreams were coming true. We were all out here living our very best lives, young, rich, and flourishing.

Today was our first round of radio interviews, starting with Houston's most popular radio show, *The Three Peas Morning Show*. I'd listened to these clowns in the car on most of my morning commutes. And it was surreal to think that I'd be sitting in the same seats that Plus, Pimp C, and every member of Destiny's Child, past *and* present, had sat in.

They'd split me and my four bandmates into groups, sending Kimi and Jock to their sister station while me, Bre and Sabre chopped it up with *TTP*. Everybody pretended not to know why Jock was being sent in the opposite direction as me and Bre, but obviously, we all knew what was up. It had been about two weeks since the blow-up at Bottoms, and though it was apparent that Kenny wanted to wring Jock's neck it would be better for publicity and more cost-effective to let things die down until we wrapped this tour.

Our sets had been altered in a way that would look seamless to the audience. Kenny got with JT and made it so that Jock didn't have to be at rehearsals at the same time as me and Bre. And if he showed up, he'd be replaced like Latoya and Latavia. I hated that things had to be so awkward with *The Crew*, knowing that it was half my fault for dating another member of the group. But it was what it was. Shit happens sometimes. Perfect picture or not, the show had to go on.

"You good?" Sabre finally asked after staring at me like a registered nurse for the ten minutes we'd been sitting in the waiting area.

"Yeah. Why wouldn't I be?" I looked up from my phone, smirking.

"Because you're staring at that phone like it has the answer to the meaning of life." Bre chimed in, popping her lips after smearing bubble gum lip gloss on them.

"I was gonna say you look worried." Sabre shook his head at Bre, bringing his eyes back to me. "Interviews can be nerve-racking. Just making sure you're ok."

"Thanks, Sabe. But I'm good." I took a deep breath in then blew it out, totally contradicting everything I'd just said.

"You know what would make you feel better?" Bre acted like she didn't just hear me say I was fine. "If you'd call him instead of waiting for him to call you."

"Call who?" Sabre asked.

"Your boy, Chad," Bre replied, dropping her lip gloss in a purse that could easily house a family of four.

"And don't look at me like that." She smacked her lips, long nails clicking together as she pulled her words together in front of her like she always did.

"Wait, Chad didn't called you?" Sabre sounded surprised. Almost as if he'd told his friend to hit me up out of pity when I knew damn well he wouldn't do anything that stupid.

"First of all, he doesn't need to." I rolled my eyes at Bre. "And second," I slid my focus back to Sabre who looked just like himself in a pair of jeans, loafers and a vest over a white T-shirt. "Please tell me you didn't tell him that he needs to."

"I umm..." Sabre stuttered.

"Sabre, seriously?" I whined. "Do you know how embarrassing this is? How embarrassing it's gonna be when or *if* we ever see each other again? I don't need his sympathy. He's not interested. I can accept rejection. I'm not a child."

"Nobody said you were a child, Tay. I was just tryna help." Sabre explained.

"Yeah, well, you didn't." I shook my head, rolling my eyes up to the ceiling, quickly yanked out of my feelings when the door swung open.

"Alright, you guys ready?" The chipper receptionist, Paula, peeped in with a clipboard tucked under her arm and a smile on her face as wide as Lizzo's hips.

The three of us stood at the same time, Bre managing to do so on a pair of thigh-high suede boots with heels that took her from five feet ten inches to damn near six three. The short trip down the hallway to the studio seemed to go on forever with all the thoughts running through my mind.

Had the stylist dressed us appropriately?

Did we look too matchy with our fall ensembles?

Which one of us would be the target of Lem and Squeeze's jokes?

Had any news from the incident at Bottoms spilled that could turn this whole interview into a shit show?

"Taya?" Bre nudged me as we approached the studio door. "Go, girl." She pressed a hand against my back and pushed me forward. I don't know why they always wanted to me to enter first.

Something about me being the face of *The Crew*, which didn't make sense to me and probably never would.

But I went in, tugging at the bottom of my dark blue jean jacket that was left open to expose the red camisole beneath tucked into a pair of brown gauchos that flowed over tan pumps. All three hosts stood and greeted us before showing us to our seats, and I was taken aback by how beautiful Jada, the female portion of the trio, was in person. Of course, once I got past her beauty, I was quickly reminded that she was the older sister of the man who'd protected and rejected me just a few weeks prior. I wondered if he'd told her about me. If he'd mentioned my desperation over dinner and laughed about it with the rest of their family. God, why was I even here? I was about to get blasted for being a stupid girl running to the arms of a stranger after a public fall out with my ex. I should've told Kenny I wasn't feeling well and got out of this shit. But it was too late for that now. My behind was in a chair between two of my bandmates.

"What up, Yewston?!" Lem's intro made me straighten in my seat. It was hard not to smile with him disrespecting my city's name like that.

"It's ya boy, Lem, with Squeeze,"

"Aye!" Squeeze spoke.

"Jada,"

"Good morning!" Jada chirped.

"And you know this is the TTP Morning Show!"

The applause track sounded just like it had for the last few years since Lem, Squeeze and Jada took over the show. And, in keeping with the flow of things, Lem went into his daily rantings about events that had transpired over the weekend. I sat between Sabre and Bre, nervously shaking my leg under the table, praying to God that nothing had spilled or so help me God, I would've melted into the floor. And when Lem made it to the end of his segment without mentioning mine or Jock's names, I breathed a sigh of relief, and my leg stopped moving on its own.

"Aight, y'all. We got some young, beautiful, gifted and talented guests in the building this morning." Lem announced, panning his eyes across the table at the three of us for the first time since we sat down. "And in my opinion, they're too young to be making this much money. I mean I was dead broke in my early twenties. I'm talkin' ramen noodles with weenies in 'em six days a week."

"You talkin bout Ball Parks?" Squeeze, leaned forward, closer to his mic, fat face spreading into a smile.

"Hell nah," Lem replied. "I'm talkin' bout them eighty-nine cent joints. Ain't even have a real name on em. The stocker just wrote *'skinny meat logs'* on the package with a permanent marker." Lem said with a serious face.

"You stupid." Jada busted out laughing. "Certifiably stupid." She looked at us, seemingly apologizing with her eyes for the behavior of her cohost.

"Right hand to God." Lem shifted in his seat, straightening a stack of papers sitting on the table before him. "And *meat* was in quotations so it ain't no tellin' what I was really eatin'."

At that, everybody busted out laughing. If this little segment was meant to loosen us up, it had worked for me one hundred percent.

"You said six days a week. What'd you eat on the seventh?" Squeeze inquired because, apparently, food was his favorite thing to discuss.

"You know you're the only one that caught that, right?" Lem looked at Squeeze judgingly. Jada giggled as she took a sip from her lidded drink.

Squeeze shrugged his meaty shoulders and said, "It's my job to pay attention to details."

"Specifically, *food-related* details." Jada nodded, placing her cup on the table in front of her.

"Anyway," Lem shook his head. "On the seventh day, somebody always looked out for me." The typical humor in his tone had almost completely faded away.

"Really? Who?" Jada asked.

"Nigga, you bout to *cry*?" Squeeze rested his forearms on the table and craned his neck to look sideways at Lem.

"Nah. Hell no," Lem replied. "But yeah, it was Plus." He disclosed and all of our mouths fell open, although neither of us found it hard to believe since the only reason we were even sitting in those seats was because of Kenny's desire to give back to the community that made him.

"What do you mean it was Plus?" I asked, suddenly more invested in this conversation.

"First let me clear this up," He started, big hands folded on top of the table as he looked across the space at me, Bre and Sabre. "Plus wasn't out there handing out sandwiches. I was umm..." His eyes slanted between both of his cohosts and I sensed a bit of hesitation. Like maybe things were going in a direction that he hadn't foreseen.

"Ok, so I was homeless for a minute." Lem was definitely going off-script. And apparently, their producer, Squeeze, and Jada were too intrigued to stop him.

"Yeah, surprise." He chuckled to lighten the mood. "Anyway, y'all might not know this but Plus ran a men's shelter. Like a legit spot to lay your head, wash your ass, and if you were serious about getting on your feet, they had job programs to help you do that too. The only thing different about this shelter was that you didn't eat for free Monday through Saturday. You had to work for that. I mean the meals were cheap, but you had to earn 'em and cook for yourself. But on Sundays, all you were expected to do was rest. It was the only rule. And if you got caught *not* resting on Sundays, you got roasted. It was crazy."

Squeeze squinted his eyes at Lem in total disbelief and said, "Bro, you serious?"

"Dead ass." Lem tipped his head to the side. "Went from sleeping in a Honda Civic to sleeping on a mostly comfortable futon. The place was nice."

"Lem, you're at *least* six-two," Jada observed, long layered hair pulled into a high ponytail on top of her head. "There's no way you slept in a Honda Civic without dislocating every bone in your body. No way!"

"Right hand to God." Lem raised a hand, eyes bucked for emphasis. "Looked like I was playin' one-man Twister in the back seat."

I swear, my stomach was cramping from laughing at these three. If we thought their comedic chemistry was off the charts over the airwaves, it was that times a trillion in person.

"Man, I'm not about to play with you," Jada said on the end of a laughing fit. "We're gonna take a small break and we'll be back in two with our guests. Hang tight."

The producer cut to commercial break, offering us refreshments while we prepared to be interviewed. I asked Lem if he was really serious about Plus running a men's shelter and he swore on a literal Bible that Jada handed him from her workstation, that he was telling the whole truth.

Once the commercial wrapped, we put our serious faces on since this interview would be streaming live on all TTP's social media sites and ours as well. We answered questions about tour dates, the dynamic of our relationships, and how it was living with virtual strangers during our days at *Plus Academy*. These were easy questions to answer between the three of us since we all got along like sisters and brothers. But when Squeeze brought up the two members who'd gone to their sister station, things got a little bit heated.

"So, what's up with you and Jock?" He looked straight at me and had I been a few shades lighter, my cheeks would've turned red.

Sabre and Bre sat beside me, pretending to be preoccupied with drinking from damn near empty water bottles, leaving me sitting there looking like a deer caught in headlights. But then I remembered who I was, and more importantly *whose* I was. No daughter of Tashena Maxey would be ruffled by such a simple question.

"Well, I'm sure all your female listeners will be happy to know that there is no longer a me and Jock." I smiled, somewhat relieved at the feeling of saying that out loud.

"Oh really?" Jada curiously questioned. "When did this happen? Y'all looked so cute together."

"Looks can be deceiving." I planted my elbow on the armrest of my chair. Bre elbowed me hard as hell like I'd said something I shouldn't.

"Elaborate." Now Squeeze was intrigued. "Jock got moles in strange places or somethin'? You know light-skinned dudes come with ailments."

Sabre shook his head and Bre covered her mouth to stop from spitting her water out.

"No. It was nothing like that." I giggled. "We just didn't work. Some stuff is better in theory." Those words sounded like lyrics, so I pulled out my cell and wrote them in my note app.

"I see you youngin, spittin' that old school wisdom." Lem offered a nod of approval. Then we ended our session with a few more laughs and the playing of our latest hit single, *"On"*.

I'd sat across the table from Jada waiting for my turn to take a selfie. I don't know why I was so nervous since she and the other two-thirds of *TTP* made us feel like family. But when she asked to speak with me in private after the last segment wrapped, I couldn't help wondering why. Actually, I had an idea why and didn't know how to respond.

"Come on in." She was so easy going, pushing the door open to a fairly small office decorated in pink and yellow stationery, wall art, and so many pictures of her family.

One picture, in particular, caught my eye and kept it. A young Chad, no older than twelve, posing in one of those staged photos on a baseball mound, resting a bat on his shoulder, trying his best to scowl like Jacky Robinson with the perfect athletic posture. He was gorgeous even then. The only difference was the structure of masculinity that now adorned his face.

"*That* boy." Jada's soft but authoritative voice pulled my eyes away from Chad's photo as she looked up from her seat behind a small, winter white desk, wearing a proud smile. "That picture's as fake as the ivory hanging over my window. Chad couldn't swing a bat to save his life." She giggled.

"Then why'd he take the picture?" I smiled at the thought of him being bad at anything.

"For girls, mostly." She curved her lips. "He had Daddy sign him up, pay for registration and everything, all for him to quit the team after picture day. It was pitiful." She was laughing again and I was laughing right along with her. "Also, this is the only picture left after he destroyed them to hide evidence of how far he'd go to impress a girl. Consider yourself sworn into secrecy!"

After the laughter subsided I just stood there silently, taking in the rest of the pictures trying to figure out a way to ask her what this was about.

"I'm so sorry. Have a seat." She swept a hand toward the chair directly across from her desk. And I don't know how she knew I was thirsty, but she reached into a mini-fridge beneath her window seal, grabbed two bottles of water and handed one to me.

"Okay, so, I know your time is limited." She started, after we both took sips from our water, mine more of a nervous gulp. "So, I'm just gonna cut to the chase. This is about my brother."

"*Lord*. Did he put you up to this?" I pretended not to be flattered by the thought. "'Cause if he did, you're wasting your time. He had his chance and he blew it. Left me standing in the middle of the sidewalk looking stupid in front of my friends. You know how embarrassing that was?"

"No, I don't." She plainly replied. "And I'm sorry that happened to you."

"Well, that's nice. And I appreciate it. But with all due respect, you can't speak for your brother. He's a grown man and he should—"

"Jay, this better be important. I still got stuff to do up here before five and you blowin' up my…*Taya?*" Chad had backed his way into Jada's office and made his way through half a rant before turning around and noticing that his sister had company.

"Well, here he is." Jada stood and rounded her desk. "Her folks leave in ten minutes." She said to Chad. "Security's gonna bust thru that door if y'all haven't wrapped it up by then. Good luck!" She tapped me on the shoulder, grabbing the baseball picture of Chad off her bookshelf before offering the same shoulder pat to him on her way out of the door that she pulled closed behind her.

"I'm sorry. I didn't know she was gonna do this."

I expected Taya to yell at me, slap my face, maybe even call me a trifling piece of shit. But she didn't do any of that. Just stood from her seat, flipped those braids over her shoulders and walked toward the door that I was still standing in front of.

"Excuse me." She said without giving me her eyes. And surprisingly that hurt more than being slapped in the face.

"Can we talk?" I directed my words down to the tip of her round nose.

"I have somewhere to be." She returned stiffly, still not giving me her eyes.

"In…" I looked over her shoulder at the two-sided analog clock on Jada's desk. "Six minutes."

She pushed out a deep breath and said "Fine." folding her arms across her chest, finally giving me her eyes validating the fact that all the apologizing I might have to do would be worth it.

"You wanna sit?" I angled my body toward the set of chairs beside the door.

"I'm fine." She snapped.

"Cool." I stuffed my hands in my pockets, mouth suddenly dry as hell. "So, I heard the show down in the break room. It was nice. Y'all did good."

"Look, if you wanna do a recap of the show, just hit up Sabre. I don't have time for this." She tried brushing past me but I stopped her by grabbing her hand.

"I'm sorry." I looked down at our hand and released when she pulled away. "I didn't mean to—"

"There are probably a lot of things you don't mean to do, Chad. But you do them anyway. And in the past, you've probably just apologized and moved on. Because you're, I don't know, covered by the blood of the lamb or something. But that's not gonna happen today. Now, please move so I can go."

On a deep sigh that had me swallowing my pride and everything else, I stepped aside as requested. I rested a sweaty palm on the doorknob, and before turning it, I said, "I'm not the one you should be mad at."

"What?" She squinted, looking sideways and up into my face.

"I didn't come at you sideways. I didn't disrespect you in any kinda way. I just wanted to make sure you were ok. If that makes me a bad person, so be it."

"This is… *Wow!*" She rubbed a hand up her forehead and shot her eyes to the ceiling. "You really are a professional bull shitter." She squinted at me. "Do you have selective memory or something?

You left. I asked if you had me and you responded by leaving. That's the opposite of making sure I was ok."

"You were in good hands."

"I was on a sidewalk looking like an idiot in front of my friends!" She yelled. And I was sure security heard us on the other side of the door.

That assumption was validated when Cha Cha pushed the door open. My eyes swept between the two women before I said, "I'm sorry if—"

"There is no *if*." She sliced through my words, raw emotions boiling just beneath the surface of her brown skin.

"Okay." I straightened my stance. "I'm sorry *that* I hurt your feelings and embarrassed you. But trust me, it was better that way."

Taya glanced at Cha Cha who was tapping her watch instead of saying *let's go* like a normal human being. "Since when are you an expert on what's best for me?" She rolled her eyes from Cha Cha to me.

"I'm not. And I didn't leave for you. I left for myself."

"You know what," She angled toward the door.

"Would you just hear me out? I got two minutes. Right, Cha Cha?"

Cha Cha looked down at her watch and nodded.

"Whatever." Taya threw a hand up in surrender and waited.

"Look, I'm not good at this… whatever's happening right now. And to be honest, I'm lost. Literally."

"I have no idea what you're talking about." A puzzled look crossed her face and even that made me want to kiss her.

"Neither do I." I sighed, eyes up to the ceiling before lowering to look at her face. "And that's the problem. At least part of the problem. Listen, I'm gonna need more than two minutes to explain this to you because obviously, I need to explain it to myself first." I was shooting my best shot and praying it fell through the net.

She was silent, seemingly lost in her thoughts, eyes still on me which I took as a good sign. I held my breath anticipating her response, which was never my thing.

What the hell was this girl doing to me?

"Are you comin' to the show tomorrow?" She stood in the doorway and asked.

"Yeah. Sabre hooked me up with some tickets. Why?"

"I'll be free for a few hours after the show. If you've figured this out by then…" She blinked then rolled her eyes away from me as she headed out the door.

Five

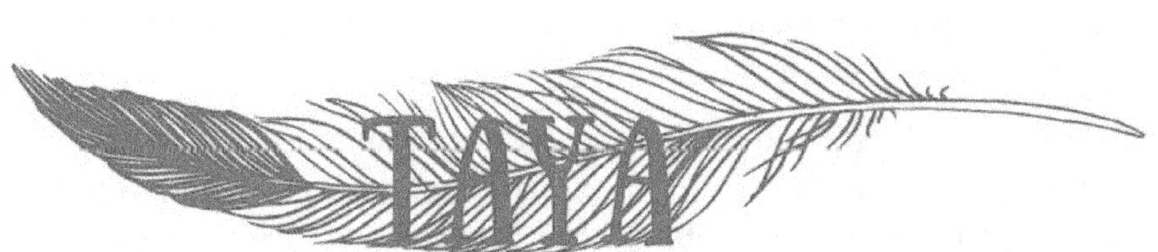

I hadn't seen my old neighbors, Bryan and Bella, since before the tour started and I missed them like crazy. Their mother, Kearston, had moved them out of the house next door to us a few weeks after Kenny convinced Mama to move in with him. There was a history at that place that Kearston couldn't live with and I didn't blame her one bit for leaving. I was glad, however, that she'd agreed to keep in touch since we'd grown a closeness with her and her kids that was bigger than what had gone down.

Before the tour kicked off, I'd mailed her tickets for every show and Kenny made sure that traveling accommodations were made too. They'd missed the first few shows due to work and school, but tonight, my little buddies were front and center, singing every lyric to every song like they'd written them themselves. Seeing them had helped to take my mind off of Chad and how bad I wanted to stay mad at him even after he'd apologized. There was a pull between us that couldn't be ignored, still, I was wise enough to know that that type of energy could be dangerous.

"Taya, I'm over here!" Bella yelled from the other end of the hallway just as I was stepping out of my dressing room. Before I could say anything, her little arms were wrapped around my waist, and her big brother Bryan wasn't far behind.

"You look so pretty!" She looked up into my eyes, little black afro forming a crown around her head with a bow tucked on the side to hold part of it behind her ear.

"Thank you, baby. You look pretty too!" I leaned in to kiss her cheek. "I missed you."

"I missed you too. I threw teddy bears onstage for you, Bre, and Kimi. Did you get 'em?" She was bouncing up and down, probably high from raiding the candy buffet that Mama'd had arranged for them backstage.

"We did." I smiled wide. "And we're gonna take them with us everywhere we go. Hey, B!" I pulled Bella to my side, reaching out an arm to embrace her lanky big brother who'd finally made his way to us.

"Wassup, Tay?" He gave the same awkward side hug that most teenage boys gave. He seemed to have grown three feet since the last time I saw him and had some structure to that handsome babyface.

"How are those grades looking?" I asked. I always asked because I knew how distracting high school girls could be, especially when you were as tall and handsome as Bryan.

"Good." He gave a one-word answer, and suddenly I missed the little ten-year-old chatterbox he used to be. "Is Bre back here?" I couldn't believe he had the nerve to ask. Granted, every teenaged boy in the whole world had a crush on my friend, I didn't know my boy Bryan could be this forward.

"She'll be out in a minute. Why? You tryna get an autograph?" I pulled my arm from around him and propped a hand on my hip.

"Nah." He rubbed the stubble on his chin. *Stubble*! I was about to come unglued. "I'm tryna get her number." He said with such confidence I had to look around to make sure it was him.

"Bryan?" I bucked my eyes at the six-foot-tall fifteen-year-old boy who used to gobble down my Mama's grilled cheese sandwiches on a daily basis. "Bre is a grown woman. You better chill."

"That's cool." He smirked, rubbing that stubble again. "In three years, I'll be a grown man. I'm just tryna shoot my shot early."

"Boy!" I thumped his shoulder, having to reach up a bit to do so. And like clockwork, Bre came strutting over in a pair of sneakers, sweats, and hoodie, which was typical attire after we'd sweated our edges out on stage.

"Hey! This must be Bryan and Bella." She chirped, and Bryan almost passed out.

"Bryan has a girlfriend!" Bella snitched, gripping my hand and flicking her tongue out at her brother.

"Is that right?" Bre slanted a smile from Bre to Bryan. "I was just about to ask how old he was."

"No, I don't!" Bryan yelled at Bella. "And I'll be eighteen in three years. You wanna gimme your number so I can hold on to it til then?"

The boy licked his lips like LL Cool J and winked at Bre like there was a chance in hell of her giving him even one digit from her phone number.

"I'll tell you what, B. Can I call you B?" Bre asked, grabbing ahold of Bryan's hand and causing every hair on his pubescent body to stand on end, I'm sure.

"Yeah. Yes, ma'am. I mean…*yeah*." My boy was struggling to catch his breath all of a sudden.

"How about we take a pic together?" Bre suggested. "That way all the girls at school can see what you're capable of pulling. I promise you won't even be thinking about me when those DM's blow up."

"Oh, ok." Bryan shrugged his bony shoulders, pulling out his phone and handing it to Bre, allowing her to do what she did best, taking a million selfies in ten seconds.

"Here they go, girl." Kearston and Mama came down the hallway looking for the kids.

"Lord, are they bothering y'all?" Kearston asked, shaking her head at Bryan and Bella.

"I wasn't, Mama," Bella said, still holding my hand. "But Bryan's tryna get Bre's phone number when everybody knows he already has a girlfriend."

"Man, shut up." Bryan swatted at Bella.

"Bryan." Mama stepped in like she always did, big belly and all.

"Sorry, Miss T. She's always in my business." Bryan smacked his lips.

"You ain't got no business," Kearston smirked at him. "Sorry about that, baby. These teenage hormones or either gonna kill *me* or *him*." She smiled at Bre.

"It's all good." Bre grinned. "He was the perfect gentleman. But thanks for looking out, Bella. Us ladies gotta stick together." She winked at Bella then they exchanged high fives.

"Speaking of sticking together," Mama mentioned, slanting her eyes at me. "Somebody's waiting for you over in Sabre's dressing room. Bella, Bryan, y'all ready?" She redirected her attention to the kids.

"Where y'all goin'?" I asked, not wanting to be left out although I already had other plans.

"None of your business." Mama curved her lips.

"McKinley said we're going to a skating rink at the compound!" Bella blurted.

"Bella, you're really on the snitch train tonight, ain't you?" Mama propped a hand on her hip and bucked her eyes at Bella.

Bella giggled and stayed close to my side until it was time to say our goodbyes and their mama and mine took her and Bryan off to the compound for skating and other fun shit that I'd be missing because I'd made a promise to a man who was tangling my feelings.

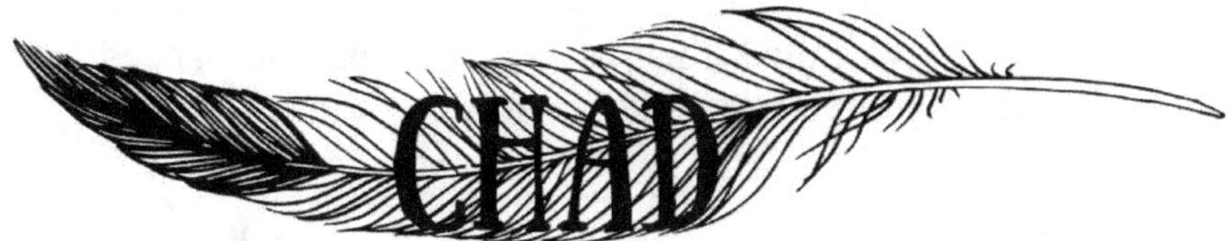

The Crew's performance was up there with some of the best. And I'd been dragged to three Beyoncé concerts with my sisters so that was definitely saying a lot. Still, it bothered me that Taya had to be on stage with Jock after what went down at Bottoms, especially since Plus was running the show. Seemed like finding another light-skinned nigga with a curly fade would've been an easy task to carry out.

In any event, the show was over, and as planned, Taya was rolling with me. Her phone had been going off since the minute her behind hit the leather seat in my truck but she didn't look down at the screen once. Just stared out the window watching the streetlights go by.

"You don't think you need to get that?" I asked, eyes leaving the road for a millisecond to take in the unbothered look on her face.

"No." She replied without looking at me. "It's just my mama teasing me with pictures of everybody skating back at the compound. Either that or somebody got a video of what happened at Bottoms and figured tonight would be a good time to upload it."

"Word? You wanna go over there?" I offered.

"Nah, I'm good." She took a deep breath and blew out. And suddenly, I was convinced that she didn't wanna be anywhere near me.

"What if they're checkin' up on you? Can't believe security just let you leave with me like that." I gripped the steering wheel, signaling right at the intersection, trying hard to dismiss the thought that she'd come along with me out of pity.

"You see that black Hummer in your rearview?" She looked up at the mirror, and so did I. "That's Cha Cha. She doesn't trust anybody. And if you push this car one mile past the speed limit, the grill of that Hummer's gonna be embedded in the back of your truck."

Now she gave me her eyes and a slither of a smile to go with them.

"And if you're worried about Jock, there's a Hummer just like that one taking him home right now."

"What makes you think I'd be worried about Jock?" My brows furrowed. Shit came out of nowhere.

"Oh, nothing. Just the fact that you were mugging him backstage."

Damn, she caught that?

"It's all good." She shrugged a shoulder. "Makes sense if you're still pressed."

"Oh, I'm not pressed," I assured her. "Just concerned about your safety."

"Well…thank you." She said. "And you're not alone in that. Everybody agrees that he shoulda been kicked off the tour. But Kenny doesn't roll like that. He's not the type to give up on people."

The expression on her face said I should probably leave it at that, and I wanted to. But I couldn't.

"Y'all still dealing with each other?" I hated myself for asking.

"No." She answered without hesitation, and I breathed an undetectable sigh of relief. "Not like that, anyway. He was having a hard time taking no for an answer and I'm not good with ripping off band-aids."

"Oh." Was all I could come up with.

"My sentiments exactly." She returned, twisting a handful of braids through the tips of her fingers.

"What's the usual protocol when shit pops off? Dude seemed pretty messed up that night."

"Believe it or not, that was the first time I ever saw him get physical with anybody." She disclosed. "He's always wilding out, but it's usually just jumping in pools with all his clothes on or drinking too much and being loud for no reason. Even with all of that, he's still under contract with Plus Academy. All of us are for the duration of the tour. He's basically Plus's bitch and his safety is priority whether he wants to be safe or not. What you saw at Bottoms was him pretending he runs anything. What you *didn't* see after leaving Bottoms was his own security guard jacking him up by that tight ass shirt, and throwing him in the backseat of *Hummer Number Two*."

"So, your rides are numbered?" This stuff was intriguing.

"Do you wear glasses, bro?" She giggled. "The number's as big as day on the license plate."

I glanced in the rearview again and sure enough, there it was, *Number One,* big as day.

"Damn." I tilted my head to the side. "And actually, I do wear glasses."

"Why aren't you wearing them now?"

"Contacts." I winked. "I only wear glasses on special occasions."

"Such as?" She folded her arms across her chest, having no idea how good she looked sitting shotgun in my ride.

"You know, reading in bed, stuff like that."

"You literally named one thing!" She huffed out a chuckle, shaking her head, a rainbow of brown dancing in her eyes.

She sighed, relaxing against the seat. "Where are you takin' me anyway?"

"*Not* to read in my bed. Don't worry." I grinned.

"And why would I be worried? Who's to say *you* shouldn't be worried?"

"Cute," I smirked, pulling into the reserved parking spot in front of my shop.

She didn't seem amused and that cracked me up more.

With her eyes rolling in my peripheral, I killed the engine, hopped out and rounded the front of the truck, feeling her eyes on me through the windshield. I pulled her door open, catching the Hummer that had been following us from the corner of my eye. Cha Cha wasn't even trying to hide at this point. Parked right beside us and rolled the window down.

Taya accepted my hand as I helped her out of the truck, unbothered by Cha Cha creeping up on us like a streetwalker. I guess this was a part of the celeb life that she'd gotten used to. I'd been around plenty of famous people but this was always gonna be odd to me.

"Seriously?" Taya canvased the shop front, music from inside loud enough to rattle the windows.

"What, I owe you right?" I looked down the slope of my arm at her before pushing the door open, remembering that I'd offered her a free tattoo in exchange for her number the first time we met at Bottoms. "Ain't nobody gonna bother you in here, I swear. They've all had background checks. Let's go." I smiled and she followed my lead.

Kirk was the first to notice me and Taya walking through the door since his was the closest station to the entrance. It was hard to hide reactions under that super light skin, and I already knew something stupid was about to fly out of his mouth.

"So, you just gon' casually stroll up in here without calling to let us know you got *the* Taya Maxey comin' through for a tatt?"

The always animated lanky negro with the curly box on top of his head didn't think twice before blurting out exactly what was on his mind.

"Boy, stop lyin'. Ain't no Taya Maxey in—*what the hell?*" The next reaction came from the second chair, Paula, respectfully known as Pomade because she was thick and didn't spread easily.

Her words, not mine.

"Excuse these minions, Miss Maxey." The first chair and biggest of all three artists, David, 'Bass' Durow stepped away from his station to greet us at the door, a bottle of cold water magically appearing in his hand. "Water?" He offered, deep ass voice rattling the wall décor.

"Umm, sure. Thanks." Taya accepted the water. Not because she was thirsty but because she was a nice person... *sometimes.*

"'Preciate it, Bass." I nodded as he bowed like an extra from 'Coming to America', backing away to his station.

"Obviously, y'all know this is Taya." I waved a palm out to display my smiling guest.

"Taya, these are the most talented tattoo artist Houston has to offer. Over there is Kirk," I pointed to the dude who hadn't stopped smiling since we walked through the door.

"Paula," The ladies did some kind of synchronized girl power lip smirk that made me nervous for some reason.

"And Bass." I wrapped the introductions. From there, Taya rationed out hugs like she'd known my folks her whole life. I figured it was probably settings like this that showed who she really was. Not the spoiled little princess that the media had portrayed her to be.

"So, you gon' let Chad do your tatt or you want an actual professional to do it?" Kirk's mouth led most of his actions no matter who he was talking to.

"Actually, he owes me," Taya replied, looking up to the side at me.

"Oh!" Paula grabbed the air with her hands and pulled it in

with the tips of her fingers, returning to her customer that had been sitting there with his mouth open. "What'd you give him, sis? Chad don't do nothin' on credit."

"And I mean *nothin'!*" Kirk added, heading over to the printer to grab his client's stencil. The dude in Kirk's chair was a regular who saw celebs coming in and out of our shop so often that Taya was just another face in the crowd to him. He didn't even look up from his phone.

"I didn't give him anything, actually," Taya replied. "Guess I'm just special." She smiled at me before taking in the *oohs* and *awes* from my messy ass employees.

"Well, is she *special*, Chad?" Bass couldn't help himself. He was a sucker for love and all things love related. Brother had a library of romance novels on a small shelf mounted on the wall next to his station. "She sure seems special. You brought her in on a Saturday night. I'm not sure I've ever seen you here on a Saturday night."

"Are y'all finished?" I wasn't about to answer that question, not even with a gun to my head.

"Y'all stop." Paula came thru to save me like she always did, head full of blonde curls pulled up into a side ponytail that swept over her brows. "I'm pretty sure Taya doesn't want Chad professing his love in front of a group of strangers. It was nice meeting you, by the way. We try to have manners but it's kinda foreign." She curved her full lips to the side, signature red lipstick adding that much more animation to her already expressive face.

"It was nice meeting y'all too." Taya waved, as I led her from the main floor to my station in the back.

"So, *am* I?" It didn't surprise me at all that Taya picked that question up off the ground where I'd left it as soon as we stepped into my station toward the back of the shop.

"Are you what?" I pretended not to know what she was talking about.

"Special."

Damn.

"That question make you uncomfortable?" She perused my space, taking it all in while I literally came undone on the inside. Just watching her walk in those low-rise jeans and a loose-fitting white tank top that exposed a red bralette underneath, had my heart doing things and my breathing too.

"That question doesn't really have an answer." I pulled out a pair of black disposable latex gloves and laid them on my table. "Everybody's special, right?"

"But we're not talking about *everybody*. We're talking about *me*." Her back was still to me as she ran her fingers over all the autographed pictures of folks I'd tattooed. My clientele was ridiculous. Even I couldn't believe it sometimes, that folks had come from all over the globe to let me mark their skin.

"You know I'm just messing with you, right?" She turned around, almost catching my eyes on her behind. "I just like seeing your face do that thing." Those sexy eyes took in every crevice of my face, staring at me in a way that made a grown man blush.

"What thing?" I dared to ask, knowing full well she wouldn't be afraid to tell me.

"I could be wrong, though that's highly unlikely, but when you're nervous, you scrunch your eyebrows. You try not to, but the effort only deepens the wrinkle."

I went over that in my head for all of two seconds before accepting the fact that she was right. It's not like I was ever in front of a mirror checking for worry lines, but I could feel my brows scrunching just *thinking* about them scrunching.

"Where'd you come up with the name?" She went from picking apart my facial expressions to sitting in my chair with a leg folded under her, slits of her thighs exposed beneath ripped jeans.

"What, *Quills*?" I looked over at her. "Got a thing for feathers."

"Weirdo." She rolled her eyes, curiosity nearly getting the best of her as she craned her neck to see what I was doing at my station.

"You're really about to give me a tattoo, huh?" Her foot dangled in front of the chair wearing a pair of red sneakers from *Plus Athletics* that I'd only seen on Jet's feet because they weren't available in stores yet.

She rested an elbow on the pivoting armrest as I sat down on my stool and slid toward her after powering on the machine. "Wait! I didn't even tell you what I want yet." Those pretty browns ballooned. She pulled back her hand like she was scared I was gonna stab it. But I wouldn't. She was just fun to watch.

"So, tell me what you want." I held the needle in my left gloved hand.

"What, *right now*?"

"Yeah. You're in a tattoo parlor. What you want?"

"Chad."

"That's my name." I blinked impatiently.

"I didn't… I don't know." She blew out a breath. "Don't we have to brainstorm or something? And the stencil. What about the stencil? Please tell me you don't be up in here freestyling tatts?"

I chuckled. This girl worried about *every* damn thing.

"I don't use stencils." I gave an honest answer.

"I don't know if this is another one of your little games," She smirked. "But you ain't freestyling on this skin. Where's your book?"

"My what?"

"Your *book*. You know, the photo album where you keep all the tatts you've ever done. I wanna see it. And don't tell me you don't have one because you look like the type to keep a record of everything."

"Is that right?"

"Yes, it is. So, where's the book?" She zoomed her eyes in on me, tilting her head to the side and pursing her lips.

"I don't have a book." I slid back to my station, placed the needle on the table and powered the machine off. "But, in addition to what you see over there," I tipped my head to the framed autographed art behind her "I have a wall. Come on." I stood from the stool and headed off toward the back of the shop with her following close behind.

To the left of our supply closet was a small room with bright lighting. All four walls were almost halfway covered with pictures of tattoos that me and my team had done over the years. I'd opened up Quills when I was just twenty-two, after completing my apprenticeship under one of my college professors who worked a shop of his own on the weekends. Mom and Pops were against the whole idea for obvious reasons, but when they noticed the rapid growth in my following and realized I was gonna go for it with or without their support, they put their funds behind me and the rest was inked history.

"Wow!" Taya's mouth fell open the same way most customers' did when she saw the huge, framed picture of a multicolored quill painted on a caramel shoulder in the center of the far wall.

"Is that your work?" She asked, streaming straight to the picture and touching it as if she didn't believe it was real.

"Yeah." I nodded, joining her in front of the picture. "It's not a real tatt but it's the first piece of art I ever created in here."

"It musta been hell tracing all that. It looks so real." She was legitimately mesmerized. Would've had me blushing if I wasn't used to the attention that tat always brought.

"No tracing," I mentioned. "I told you, I don't use stencils. It's too constricting." I stood aside and allowed her to check out the rest of the pictures.

"So, you really did all this freehanded?" She peeled her eyes away from the Phoenix I'd drawn on Sabre's chest to squint at me.

"Right hand to the man." I raised my hand and grinned.

"Wow!"

"You said that already." I chuckled.

"You're talented." She nodded, taking a deep breath in. "You know what, fuck it, I'm ready." She threw her hands up in surrender before heading for the door.

"You know what you want?" I followed behind her, turning the light off and pulling the door closed behind me.

"Actually, I was thinking maybe *you* could decide." She stopped in the middle of the short hallway. I could feel the space closing around us the longer we stood still.

"You sure about that?" I stared down into her eyes, seeing things that she probably didn't intend to show me, fighting the urge to call them all out.

"Yes." The word slipped off her lips so softly that if I wasn't looking at her, I wouldn't have known she said a thing. "You seem to be pretty good at knowing what I need. Let's see if that translates to ink."

"And what's that supposed to mean?"

"Don't play crazy with me. That call back at Bottoms that left my face on the sidewalk." She sounded disappointed but that was better than upset. "I don't hold grudges, by the way. At least not for long." She took a deep breath and let her shoulders relax.

"That's why I'm here…" She added. "…in your shop when just a day ago, it was the last place I wanted to be."

"Damn, that's harsh." I frowned.

"The truth *is*, sometimes." She shrugged her shoulders.

"Then why are you here?"

She headed off toward my station as if she didn't want me to see the expression on her face when she replied, "Because I wanna be."

But I could hear it. And I felt a sense of accomplishment for earning that small drop of forgiveness.

Still, there was a challenge, and I was up for those all day. But this was something else. Taya was asking me to pick *and* place something permanent on her body, and all honesty, that shit made me nervous.

'Cause what if I drew a heart and she thought I was in love?

Or what if I drew a musical note and she thought the shit was lame?

What if I inked her initials and she thought I lacked creativity?

What if I decided not to draw anything at all and she deciphered it as a lack of confidence?

"What's wrong, you scared?" She flopped down in my chair, smiling hard and folding a leg under her again.

"If you are, I understand. I'd be scared too if somebody came at me with this proposition. Ink is permanent. One bad decision on your part and I'm stuck with it for the rest of my life. *Oh, shit*!"

She shrieked when I powered the machine back on. I slipped on a new pair of gloves and picked up my needle, then slid over in front of the pretty brown daredevil.

"Gimme your hand." I reached out, accepting the left hand she'd extended with slight hesitation.

"Do you trust me?" I asked staring straight into her eyes, no longer able to resist the urge to do so.

"A little." She bit down on her bottom lip, jumping a bit when I pressed on the foot pedal.

"That'll change." I made sure our gaze remained locked, massaging the inside of her hand, relaxing her as well as myself.

"I'm gonna touch the inside of your finger with this needle.'" I warned, still staring at her, still massaging her palm. "And when I do, don't move."

"Wait, you're gonna do it now?" She squeezed my hand.

I nodded *yes*, spreading my hand to lay her palm open.

She took a deep breath, eyes flipping up to the ceiling and lowering as she breathed out. I flashed a smile then took my eyes to the highest point that my thump had grazed and placed the needle there, leaving a barely visible black dot on the inside of her ring finger. It took less than a second but felt like an hour, being so close to her that I could feel her pulse. It was way too intimate yet not intimate enough.

"Did it hurt?"

"A little." She sucked her teeth, eyes sliding from the dot on the inside of her finger to me, a series of brown galaxies all melted into one.

"Were you scared?"

"Hell yeah!" She busted out laughing.

"What did you think I was gonna do?" I slid back to sit the needle down.

"I don't know." She spread her hand out to look at the dot again. "Is this permanent?"

"Yep." I rolled back over to her. "You like it?" I used the damp towel I'd grabbed from the table to wipe the excess ink away.

"Yeah, it's cute." She looked at it for a second, then brought her eyes to me. "How much would you typically charge for something like this?" Her voice softened in a way that would've landed my hand on her thigh and my tongue down her throat if she'd been anybody else.

But she wasn't anybody else.

She was Taya Maxey, a beautiful woman that had been the center of my thoughts for longer than I was comfortable with.

"Nothin'." Was my reply. "But you do owe me a chance to gain more of your trust." Again, my lips led the way to a place I would never have traveled.

"What?" She seemed just as startled as me.

"For a bigger tatt, I mean." I tried to fix what my self-conscience had spewed out without my permission. "You gotta trust me. Trust my abilities. That's like half the process."

"Oh really?" She ran her thumb over her tatted finger. "You require this *trust* from all your customers?"

"Nah. Just you," I answered quickly, stuck in place on the stool, right in front of her leg, so close that the warmth from her body had traveled to mine.

"Ok." She sighed. "So how do you do that?"

"I should be asking *you* that." I slid my stool back, overwhelmed by the things my heart was doing in my chest. "But in my professional opinion, dinner and a movie would be a nice start."

I knew she could have anything in the world. But something about Taya told me that she didn't want half of that shit. She took a deep breath and blew out as I walked away to start cleaning my space. A moment later I looked up to find her out of the chair and heading toward the door. I knew I was dealing with something different every time she opened her mouth. But if she walked out that door without securing a date, I wasn't sure I'd know how to take it.

"I won't be back in Houston for at least four weeks." She'd stopped in the doorway and turned around to face me. "I'm not sure what your schedule's like but we'll have a rest day between a couple of shows. I can shoot you the itinerary if you want."

"Yeah, that's… that'd be cool." I stood up straight, dropping a handful of plastics and paper towels in the trash can thinking to myself how hard it was becoming to play it cool in her presence.

"Cool." She nodded, an awkward smile crossing her face "I'll text you as soon as I get settled in. And Chad." She paused, the sound of my name so light on the bed of her tongue. Like she was tasting it to see if it had the right amount of ingredients.

"Yeah." I stood there, unable to move out of fear that I might stumble from being too eager.

I was *not* myself.

"Thanks for the tatt. You did pretty good without a stencil." She smiled again, less awkward this time. Then Cha Cha looked down at her watch and I knew what time it was.

Six

A tight work schedule wouldn't allow me to fly out to Florida like I'd wanted during *The Crew's* third stop on *The First Semester* tour. The most I'd heard from Taya was a text here and there. I could've put in more effort but I didn't wanna be a pest. Sabre'd told me they were barely sleeping between shows, averaging four hours downtime a day. I don't know how they even had time to take a dump between all that. But from the looks of their social media posts, they were turning all the way up.

I'd just settled in after a day at the radio station working an accounting gig that was supposed to be temporary but had lasted a whole year. I wasn't physically tired, but it was the middle of the week. With no appointments at Quills, it was time for take-out and chill.

I'd put on my glasses, preparing to research calligraphy since I had a bridal party coming in in a couple of weeks that wanted their names inked on the insides of their fingers. It seemed simple enough in theory, but it was new territory for me. A few goes with a banana and I'd be ready though. No stencils. No worries. Just

73

perfection and nothing less.

Just as I started to fall down the rabbit hole of calligraphy videos on YouTube, my cell vibrated on the nightstand and I was surprised as hell to see Taya's face on the screen. And it wasn't just her face that surprised me. It was the fact that there was no makeup on it and her braids were wrapped in a red hair bonnet. Yet she still managed to be strikingly gorgeous. This shit wasn't even fair.

I cleared my throat and answered the call, "Hey." I tried to sound cool but there was no way to pull that off when all I wanted to do was take her damn lips into my mouth.

"Wassup, Egon? Did I wake you?" Her smile spread from one end of the screen to the other. I pushed my glasses up the brim of my nose, surprised that she knew the name of one of the Ghostbusters.

"No. And I see you got jokes." I smiled back, closing my laptop and resting my back against the headboard.

"Always!" She giggled.

"Well, you shouldn't. Lookin' like a hood mama droppin' her kid off at school."

"Wait, you talkin' bout my Mama?"

"If the house shoe fits!" I laughed and so did she, sweetest sound I'd ever heard, and already missed before it stopped.

"What you doin' in a bonnet? It's what, ten o'clock over there?" I tried hard not to stare into those eyes but they called at me.

"Yeah." She sighed, sounding disappointed. "Our second show got canceled due to bad weather. So we're all on the bus looking crazy."

"Crazy indeed." I teased.

"You know what, you got a lotta nerve sittin' behind those thick ass glasses." She rolled her eyes.

"Man, my glasses ain't that thick." I defended but didn't dare take them off or she would've been a brown blur on the screen

"Oh, but yes they are." She giggled like she'd called specifically to roast me.

But it was all good. Roasting was a sport in my household.

A beat of silence passed before she sighed and asked: "What were you doing?"

"I'd tell you but I'm not tryna get roasted again." I tucked a hand behind my head and watched her smile reappear.

"Man, stop it. I'm done." She straightened her face.

"I'on't believe you. Put that on a Plus album." I joked, and she laughed.

"I was researching calligraphy." I disclosed and waited for the roasting to commence.

"You're playin' right?" Her face went flat, dim lighting from the cramped space she was sitting in highlighting her high cheekbones.

"Not at all. Got some clients comin' in a few weeks and I'm just tryna get ready."

"Oh, ok." She nodded. "Thought you were about to start making calligraphy videos."

"That's not a bad idea. They're relaxing as hell."

"Ain't they?" She agreed, unwrapping a snack and biting into it.

"Real talk." I grinned. "What you eatin'?"

"An oatmeal pie." She was smacking, wrapper crinkling in her hand.

"Throwback snack." I leaned my phone back to see who was calling.

Unknown.

"Throwback indeed. I stole it from my mama's stash. You need to get that?" She held a tiny piece of pie between her fingers.

"Nah, I'm good." I swiped the call away and crossed my feet at the ankles.

Comfortable was the tone of the next couple of hours We chopped it up like old friends with a few appearances from Bre, Sabre, and the infamous Kimi Wells popping in to give Taya a hard time. I didn't ask Taya where Jock was since Sabre'd already told me he'd mostly secluded himself from the pack, choosing to sleep toward the front of the bus to keep drama to a minimum. My only wish was that I could've been sitting next to her instead. The energy was crazy, validating things I'd questioned. It was no coincidence that we'd crossed paths. This shit right here was kismet.

"So, you wanna hit me back tomorrow or somethin'? I know you need your sleep." The last thing I wanted to do was hang up. But we weren't kids. We both had things to do when the sun came up.

She didn't answer right away, but as I stared at the screen waiting for her reply, I could see the wheels turning in those pretty brown eyes.

"You're gonna roast me for saying this," She finally spoke up, lips caught somewhere between a smile and a frown.

"*Probably*. But say it anyway." I teased, though roasting seemed to be the most effective escape from showing how bad I had it for this girl.

She shook her head, smiled then breathed out a sigh. "My mama was strict growing up, her and my aunt. And I didn't have the same experiences as my friends and peers 'cause I was too busy with dance rehearsals or voice coaching or SAT preps in case the first two didn't work out."

She paused and looked at me, I'm guessing to see if I was still listening.

And I was.

To my surprise and anybody else's, I'd been listening and talking to her for three solid hours and wouldn't have known how much time was passing had it not been for Sabre and Bre dropping reminders in our group texts every thirty minutes.

"Not to sound like an after school special—"

"Damn, you remember those?" I interjected.

"Had em on DVD." She laughed. "Another depressing part of my childhood." This time I laughed.

"Anyway, what I'm tryna say is that I like this. I like *you*. And if it's not too much, I wanna ask you a favor."

"Shoot." I tipped my chin up as she chewed the inside of her lip, having no idea that if she asked me to lasso the moon and pull it out of the sky, I'd be at Lowe's looking for rope.

"Fall asleep on the phone with me." She said. "I know it's lame and we're old as hell. But I never got to—"

"Fine." I cut her off. "I'll do it. And I don't know who you're callin' old, but I'm keeping my youth intact for at least the next seventy-five years."

"Seriously?" She giggled, a sound that had literally become my favorite overnight.

"Hell yeah." I squinted. "Me and my great-great grands are gonna be the same age at heart."

"So, you want kids?" She propped the side of her head on her fist.

"A house full." I folded an arm across my chest.

"God bless your wife." She smirked, and I knew what was coming next. "Can't imagine anybody giving birth to one, let alone a house full of babies, with heads as big as yours."

That statement sparked another hour and a half of roasting, talking, and laughing until we cried until our eyes were falling shut and we were too exhausted to speak. I'd never done this falling asleep on the phone thing either, for completely different reasons. But it was as close as I could get to falling asleep next to Taya, and for that reason alone, it didn't seem like a bad idea.

Seven

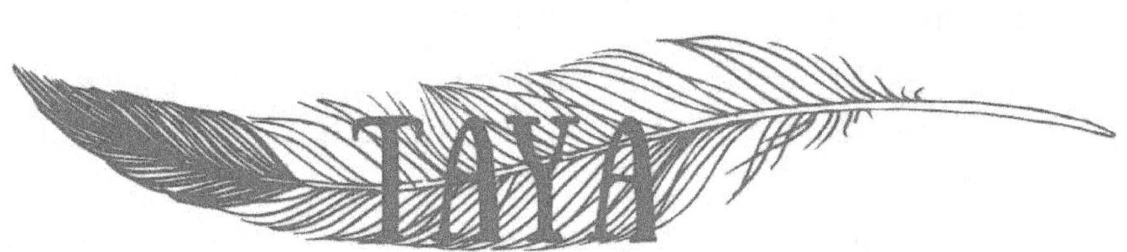

I woke up the next morning to a bullhorn blaring in my ear and the sounds of Bre, Sabre, and Kimi dying laughing next to my bunk, reminding me that I had, in fact, fallen asleep on the phone with Chad. While they called me names and threatened to reenroll me in Junior High, I couldn't help staring at Chad's handsome face on the screen. His short locs were smooshed on one side from lying on the pillow, but he was taking it like a champ instead of getting embarrassed and hanging up.

"We brought you breakfast, Sleeping Beauty!" Bre pointed to an IHOP bag on the tiny breakfast table across from our bunks after the three of them had calmed down and got out of my face.

"Where's everybody else?" I sat up, yawned, stretched and peeped around the privacy curtain to see that the bus was empty aside from the three people who'd just tried to bullhorn me to death.

"They're inside eating." Kimi tickled the bottom of my foot, long jet black hair pulled into a ponytail on top of her head.

"I think Jock's at the liquor store," Bre couldn't help herself. "Probably crying into a bottle of Wild Turkey since you were up phone boning with another nigga all night."

"Hey, I'm 'bout to hit the shower." Chad's voice startled me. I'd forgotten he was on the phone.

"Shit." I picked up the phone. "Ok. Talk to you later." I said before ending the call and rolling my eyes at Bre.

"What?" She piped.

"You get on my nerves, that's what." I climbed out of bed. "And wasn't nobody phone bonin'." I elbowed the side of her arm on my way to the restroom at the back of the bus to empty my bladder.

"Well, I woulda been. His voice is definitely phone bone-worthy." This fool had followed me to the restroom and was leaning against the wall outside the door.

"You need to get laid!" I yelled from the toilet.

"As do you!" She returned on a chuckle. "Out here behaving like a fifth-grader instead of a grown woman."

I finished up, washed my hands, stepped out of the restroom and said "I was not acting like a fifth-grader. The conversation got good and we lost track of time."

"And what were y'all talkin' about, B2K?" She teased as I brushed past her in route to the warm stack of pancakes waiting for me on the small breakfast table.

"Did I already tell you that you get on my nerves?" I took a seat in the rounded booth and popped the lid off my food, stomach waking up at the smell of crispy bacon.

"You did." She laughed, snatching a strip of bacon off my plate. "But real talk, y'all are cute." She smacked loud like always.

"There is no *we*, cow." I spread a square of butter over my pancakes. "You and I both know I don't have time for that."

"You had time last night." Kimi came skipping down the walkway with a journal full of rhymes in her hand.

"So when do I get to meet him? Heard he got that whole John David Washington vibe goin' on." Kimi opened her journal and turned to an empty page.

Bre shook her head and waited for me to respond, and when I didn't, she chimed in. "He do, Kim." She smacked her bacon-greased lips and flipped her eyes from me to Kimi. "I ain't never seen a brother look good with or without a beard. If Taya don't cuff him, I might have to add him to the roster."

"What roster?" Now Sabre had reappeared, bumping my hip and sliding into the cramped booth that wasn't meant to hold four people.

"Don't play, Sabe. You know Bre got a deck of fellas to shuffle through." Kimi winked at Bre before the two of them shared a high-five sitting side by side.

"Pssh, I ain't never seen em." Sabre hunched his shoulders, and something about his tone made me extremely curious.

I declined to speak on it until I had concrete proof. But there was definitely something brewing between him and Bre. Something they didn't want me to see.

"Anyway, let's stay focused. Taya and new bae are the topic of discussion right now." Bre nudged Kimi. "When's he comin' out? Sabre, you got any intel?"

"That's none of my business." Sabre peeped up from his phone after checking a notification.

"But that's your boy, right? He'd tell you if he was falling in love?" Bre kept going while Kimi grinned and started writing in her journal.

"Nobody's telling anybody anything because we're just friends if *that*." I cut in. "Now could y'all move so I can finish my breakfast in peace?" I scanned my eyes over three of the most annoying people I'd ever met.

They all sat there in silence looking crazy for a few seconds before collectively deciding to get up and leave me be.

I'd made it through all my scrambled eggs and one pancake before the door to the bus opened and Jock walked in. Kimi, Sabre, and Bre were outside the bus playing catch in whatever lot we were parked in, and I prayed he wouldn't come back and talk to me, but felt that it was bound to happen. I popped the lid over the food I had left, planning to make a smooth dash to the overhead storage to grab my shoes and head outside. But he noticed and made it to me before I left the booth, slid in beside me and rested his hands on top of the table.

"I'm sorry." He said, tilting his head sideways and looking at me. "I shot you and Bre a text saying that already but I'm assuming you didn't get it since you haven't replied."

"Jock, I don't—"

"I know you don't wanna talk." He cut me off. "They got you treatin' me like I'mma ghost and shit. And that's cool. I fucked up. I *know* I fucked up. And I'm sorry. That's all I wanted to say. Enjoy the rest of your breakfast."

He slid out of the booth and stood up, blue jumpsuit falling over his slender frame like it had been tailored to fit him, contrasting with his golden skin tone. It was no wonder I'd fallen for him so fast at first. There were certain things I couldn't see because the surface was so distracting.

"I got it," I spoke to the back of him as he approached his bunk at the front of the bus. "And thank you. I didn't respond because I didn't know what to say. This shit is awkward. I don't hate you but I don't know who I'm supposed to be to you."

"I'on't know either." He turned around and shrugged his shoulders. "But it ain't this."

"And what is *this*?" I squinted.

"Damn near a stranger." He huffed. "I'd say you could offer

friendship but you probably got enough of that already."

The hostility in his voice, though subtle, couldn't be ignored. So, I asked, "What's that supposed to mean?"

"You know what it means, Taya. A nigga'd have to be deaf not to hear you giggling on the phone all night."

"Oh, that…"

"Yeah *that*. And don't get it twisted, I'm not hatin'."

"You sure?" I grinned, folding a foot under me and popping the lid back off my food. "Cause it sounds like—"

"Chill, man." Now he was smiling, an expression I hadn't seen on his face in a while.

"Ain't nobody jealous of that corny *Proton Pack* shit y'all was talkin' about." He braced his palm on one of the overhead compartments, popping his compartment open and grabbing a pair of tennis shoes.

"I don't know why you insist on hating on the Ghost Busters, but it really looks bad on you." I shook my head, forking a wedge of pancakes into my mouth.

"The only good thing about the Ghost Busters was Bobby Brown's feature on the soundtrack." He chuckled before I balled up a napkin and threw it at him.

"You know I'm right." He caught the napkin and threw it back, landing it right on top of my pancakes.

"Halfway right." I popped the lid on for good this time as he took a seat on my bunk across from the table and started putting on his shoes.

"Bobby Brown did what he had to do on that track," I admitted, watching his shoulders tense as he bent forward to tighten his laces. But instead of seeing the strength in them, all I saw was the tension they carried because of things he wouldn't let go.

"Damn right he did." Jock breathed out, sitting up and resting his elbows on his thighs after tying his shoes.

We stared at each other without speaking for a second, and it was the most peaceful second we'd shared since I decided we shouldn't be together. Everybody around us knew that we were doomed before we started. But because of who I was and because of whose I was, other people's advice was no substitute for a learned lesson.

"Are we good?" He asked, and that made me smile. The fact that he even cared meant more than he could know.

"Always," I replied, extending a hand for him to shake. He planted a kiss on it instead then looked up into my eyes.

"Can you do me a favor, though?" He asked, slowly releasing my hand. I nodded *yes*.

"If you and old boy are gonna be on the phone again tonight, could you please take that shit in the restroom?"

"Hater!" I yelled as he hopped up and headed for the door.

"You niggas is lame!" He shouted back on his way down the steps and off the bus.

Eight

It had been too long and not long enough since the last time I sat down and had a talk with my mother that wasn't rushed and drenched in avoidance. I loved her, missed her, and still needed her as much as I had as a little boy. But there was so much for us to unpack that the thought of it made me tired.

Of the three of us, Jada had been the only one of our mother's children to move past mama's indiscretions and resume the normalcy of their relationship. The two of them shared a closeness that somehow overrode the pains of divorce. Me and Penny were having a harder time, with Penny's admittedly being the hardest. Even with the church moving on from our parents' public separation, we struggled on a daily basis.

It had been tradition in our family to spend second Sundays after church with Mama, just talking, watching movies or doing whatever we liked. Pops would be away on church retreats, mentoring or taking part in activities with the Men's Ministry. Since the divorce, Jada'd been the only one still spending those

Sundays with Mama. I'd send cards, flowers or gifts even though I knew that wasn't enough. But it was better than doing nothing, which was what Penny had settled on doing. At least that's what I kept telling myself so I could sleep at night.

On this particular Sunday, Penny had asked me to swing by Mama's to pick up Boogie who'd spent the weekend. I agreed, figuring I could just step in, say hello, grab my niece and cut out. She'd have Jada there as a distraction and wouldn't want me getting Boogie home too late out of fear that Penny might deny her *Granny Ma* privileges like she'd threatened to do before.

But I was wrong.

Had greatly underestimated how much my mother missed my company. When she opened the door and the smell of sweet potato pie hit my nostrils, I knew it was a trap. It wasn't even Thanksgiving.

"Unkie Chad!" Boogie came bustling down the hallway, roping her arms around my leg until I bent to pick her up.

Mama stood there smiling with her arms folded across her chest. It was crazy how youthful this lady still looked. Light brown complexion blemish-free.

"Well, somebody's happy to see you," Mama said, golden-brown eyes taking me in, probably wondering who was this cold young man and what had he done with her loving little boy.

"I hope you can stay for a little bit. I made your favorite." She added, running a hand down Boogie's back. The hopefulness in her voice making me feel bad for even thinking about turning her down.

"Yeah. I could smell it from the driveway." It was a struggle, but I kept it friendly.

And not because I hated my mother. I just hadn't been warm toward her in a long time.

"Well, come on in." She waved a hand of welcome.

"Ma, I gotta get Boogie home." I followed her down the hallway and adjusted my niece who was growing like a weed, long legs dangling down the side of me as she rested her head on my shoulder.

"You're right." She paused next to the sofa and ran a hand over the throw blanket draped over the back of it. "What was I thinking? Your sister would have a fit if you didn't get Boogie home before sundown. Let me fix you a few slices to go."

She rushed off to the kitchen just in time for Jada to emerge from the bathroom.

"Hey, brother. I thought I heard your big mouth in here." She hurried over to hug my neck, having to go around Boogie to do so. The kid was on me like white on rice.

"Wassup? Surprised you could hear me over that thunder you were droppin' in the toilet." I chuckled and Boogie's head popped up.

"Whatever." Jada elbowed me in the side.

"Tee Tee, you can make thunder just like Jesus?" Boogie's voice was lit with amazement, eyeballs as wide as the sky.

"No, baby. Your uncle's just being mean." She rolled her eyes at me then pinched Boogie's cheek before turning around to head off into the living room.

"Alright, I got you four slices in case you wanna share with somebody." Mama emerged from the kitchen with a medium-sized Tupperware bowl. "Boogie, go grab your overnight bag so Unkie Chad can get you home."

"Okay," Boogie said, hurrying off to the bedroom Mama'd designated for her the minute Penny agreed to let her visit, which took way longer than it should have.

"Wait, you're leaving already? You just got here." Jada looked over at me from her seat on one of Mama's comfy sofas. It was crazy how this house felt like home even though I'd never slept in it.

"It's okay." Mama went over and took a seat beside Jada. "You know how your sister is. Your brother will come by some other time. Won't you, Chad?"

It was fine until she added that last part. I didn't need her pressuring me. I'd come around when I was ready.

But "Yes ma'am." Was my response because *manners*.

"*Or*," Jada chimed in without being asked to. "*I* could take Boogie home and you two could do some catching up."

I didn't say anything because what the hell was I supposed to say? I guess Mama noticed my discomfort and decided to speak in my place. "I'm sure he has work in the morning, Jadalynn."

"Quills is closed on Mondays." Jada quickly retorted. "*And* he's also off from the radio station." Her eyes slanted between me and Mama, completely dismissing the fact that I wasn't ready for this shit.

You can't force somebody to have a conversation that they're not ready to have. This was all about timing and now wasn't the time.

Or was it?

Hell, would it ever be?

Had I gotten so comfortable not speaking to my mother that it had become my new normal? Would I eventually look back to find that I'd spent so much time waiting that there was no time left?

"You ready, Unkie Chad?" Boogie came out of her room with a bright pink size appropriate duffle bag slung over her little shoulder.

My eyes slid from her to Mama, to Jada before I said "Nah Boogie. Tee Tee Jada's gonna take you home."

Then she collected her hugs and kisses from me and Mama and headed out the door with her auntie.

"You want something to drink? I've got water, tea. Oh and

lemonade. I could make that little citrus tea you used to like. Remember that?"

Mama'd always gone out of her way to make everybody happy. It was probably how she wound up married to Pops for so long, suppressing who she really was.

"No, ma'am. I'm good." I stood beside the sofa, nearly stuck in place.

"Oh, ok. You um, you wanna sit down?" I hated that she sounded so nervous. Like I was a bomb she didn't wanna detonate. But I knew that was all my fault.

Instead of saying anything, I rounded the sofa and took a seat, not surprised at all by how well the cushions conformed to my frame. Mama was always on point when it came to choosing furniture. I can remember having my first growth spurt the summer before my first year of Junior High. I must've grown four inches in those three months, and the twin bed that had been good enough before now looked like a crib fit for an infant. Mama took me to some furniture store that I can't remember the name of, saying I needed to try on a bed just like I needed to try on shoes and clothes. Two hours and twelve minutes after walking into that store, we walked out with a full-sized pillow top mattress that would change the course of my sleep regimen for the duration of my teenage years.

"So, how have things been at the shop?" Small talk was never Mama's thing, but I hadn't given her much of a choice.

"It's been good," I replied as she sat down next to me, folding a leg under her like she did when she was nervous, instantly reminding me of someone else I knew.

"That's good." She nodded. "Really good. Did you ever get those pictures framed? I remember you saying you didn't know if you'd have space for 'em."

"Yeah. Yes, ma'am. I did." I said. "Found a little space in this room by the supply closet. We were gonna use it for a fifth artist but I think we're solid with four."

"Nice!" She offered a genuine smile, looking so much like

Jada it was crazy. "I'd love to come by and take a look. Maybe get a real tat this time." She nudged the side of my arm, a familiar touch that had become foreign.

My face didn't show it but I wanted nothing more than to see her walk through the door of that shop. She'd be proud to see how far things had come and glad to know that her and Pops hadn't wasted their money.

But I didn't say that. Couldn't get my mouth and my thoughts to work on one accord for some reason. She mistook that as a denied request and changed the subject to avoid the pain of rejection.

"I'm glad you're doing well, baby. I don't get to tell you that as often as I'd like, but I'm really proud of you." She patted my thigh before getting up from the sofa and running a finger across her nose trying to hide the fact that my standoffishness was making her sad.

And I hated that.

This was exactly why I didn't come over in the first place. How the hell was I supposed to not react to my crying mother?

"Mama, I'm sorry." I stood up involuntarily. "I don't mean to be cold, and I'm not tryna upset you. I just don't know how to be."

"What do you mean? I'm your mother. Just be my son."

She made it sound so simple. Like her truth hadn't literally pulled the rug from under my feet.

"But how?" I asked a simple question that didn't have a simple answer.

"The same way you always have." She walked back over to me. "I'm still the same person and so are you."

"But I'm not." I shook my head. "Because of you, because of all of this, I've changed and so have you."

"How so? Because I'm a lesbian? Is there less of me to love?"

"I didn't say that."

"Well, you're implying."

"I'm not implying anything." I didn't mean to but I'd raised my voice.

"Listen, I'm sorry okay. This is just too much. It's still too soon."

"It's been two years, Chad. Two years of crying myself to sleep at night because I feel like I made the wrong choice."

"But Mama—"

"But I didn't *have* a choice." She cut me off, staring up into my eyes with tears welling in her own. "If I did, trust me, we wouldn't be standing in this space today."

"But we are," I said. "And it hurts me too. Do you know how hard it's been wanting to call you but not knowing what to say? Tryna pick sides between you, Pops and the church? It's impossible, Mama. Ain't no book on this."

"You think I don't know that, son?" Her voice hiked with emotion. "All of that is part of the reason it took me over thirty years to leave. And to tell you the truth, if I knew that me coming out would leave you standing here treating me like a stranger, I would've waited thirty more."

"That wouldn't make sense. And I would never ask you to do that."

"Why not? Everybody else was happy. Our family was happy. Why wouldn't you want that back?"

"Because *you* weren't happy." I disclosed a secret she didn't know I'd kept.

She had no idea how much I observed her and Pops over the years and how her eyes didn't light up when he entered a room. As a kid, I never picked up on it. But as a young man, it was apparent. Love wasn't something you could fake all the way through. No matter how much love they'd created, she wasn't *in* love with him and it showed.

"Chad I don't—"

"You tried," I interjected. "You did a damn good job and I appreciate you for that. But it didn't benefit us at all sticking around that long. If you didn't love Pops, you shoulda let him know sooner. We would've been fine, all of us."

"But I did love your father. I still do, very much. Love had nothing to do with me staying or leaving him. He gave me three of the greatest gifts I'd ever received and a life far better than I'd ever imagined for myself."

"But that wasn't enough? *We* weren't enough?"

"I didn't say that. Please don't…"

I backed away as she reached for my hands. And I wished the door was closer so I could run out and leave this shit behind me.

"You were always enough. Will always be enough." Her lips trembled as a tear slid down her cheek. "There's just…there was a part of me that wasn't fulfilled. I don't know how else to explain it. And I don't know how to make you understand that I still need you in my life. I'm so sorry that I made things so hard for everybody. I really and truly am."

She wept. Back bowed, hands shaking, face drenched in tears that were probably only a drop in the bucket of the ones she'd cried over the years.

And that broke me.

Pushed away all the blaming, finger-pointing, and fucks I gave about what people might think about my mother. Because honestly, I didn't care anymore and shouldn't have in the first place. This woman had sacrificed her happiness her whole life for the sake of others. And here I was giving her a hard time when I should've been the first to forgive and move forward.

Before I could talk myself out of doing the right thing, I stepped right up to my mother and pulled her into my arms. Her tiny frame shivered against me. Tears soaked the front of my shirt. I planted a kiss on top of her head and promised her it would be okay. For the next few minutes, I listened as she muffled into my chest about how she'd prayed for this moment every morning and every night, and how much she missed her one and only son. I believed every word and let her know I'd missed her too. I made a promise to be more open and that seemed to be enough to dry her tears.

I wasn't stupid enough to make promises of things going back to the way they used to be, because no matter how much I loved her, things would never be the same. She'd always known who she was, whether she shared it with us or not. But to me, she was a different woman. Not a better or worse person, just different. And I had to get used to that. I had to sit with the fact that accepting this change in her life meant I also had to accept the woman she was with. And that was gonna be hard as hell. I'd have the same struggle if Pops ever remarried.

"I don't expect any of this to be easy for you." She grabbed ahold of my hand and squeezed it tight as we walked toward the door. "But I do expect to see more of you. I miss you."

"You're right, it's not gonna be easy." I agreed. "Luckily, I miss you too."

I pulled her little frame into an embrace that warmed me to the bone. No matter what the circumstances, my mother was made of love. No family was without disagreements, and ours was no different. We'd get through this and laugh about it someday. Hopefully someday soon.

"Before you go, when are you gonna tell me about this feather on your shoulder?" She leaned against the doorjamb with her legs crossed at the ankles.

"I'll tell you about it when I'm sure it's not gonna float away." I grinned before telling her I loved her, planting a kiss on her cheek and heading out.

Nine

"Do you think it's strange that I wanna know things about my mama's rapist?"

Me and Chad had been on this FaceTime thing for a few weeks, and it was scary how comfortable I'd become in such a short amount of time. The first leg of the tour had broken me down a lot physically, but I looked forward to our talks as soon as my head hit the pillow.

Mama's belly was growing at the speed of light, so we'd been sleeping in hotels more often than on the bus. Tour life was no place for a woman six months pregnant with triplets and I'd give her one more show before she was begging to go back to Houston.

"If these are the kinds of thoughts you're having after a show, y'all might need to switch up that playlist," Chad replied to what I already knew would be an odd question to respond to.

"Shut up." I chuckled, pulling my nighttime facial supplies out of a custom toiletry bag that Chad had gifted me from his sister's line of natural products. "I'm serious."

"I am too." I looked at the screen to find him brushing his teeth, bare chest glowing and dewy after a shower. He was a tease and knew exactly what he was doing.

"Um, could you please put a shirt on?" I rolled my eyes, stealing one last peep before wetting my face to apply Angela's *Blessed Assurance Rejuvenation Mask*.

The stuff smelled heavenly. I'd been using it every night for a week and had to fight the urge to lick it off my fingers.

"Why? You gettin' distracted?" He looked at the screen and flexed his right pectoral muscle. "Dewy man nipples messin' with your concentration?"

I tried to hold a straight face, but he kept on flexing, looking at his own nipples then grinning at me. Three long seconds into this childish game, I busted out laughing and he followed suit.

"You're childish." I picked my phone up off the bathroom counter and footed to my bed, pulling my bathrobe closed as to not expose the hard nipples under my T-shirt. Though Chad was dangerously attractive and likely thought the same of me, we were keeping it strictly platonic because that was the safest thing to do.

"I've been called worse." His head emerged from the T-shirt he'd slipped on, walking down the hallway into his kitchen to grab a bottled water and a late-night snack.

"I bet." I sat on the edge of the bed and fluffed my pillow. "And you still didn't answer my question."

"Oh, you were *serious*?" He squinted, closing the frig and heading back to his bedroom. I took in the earthy color scheme that I'd seen a dozen times at this point.

"What? You think it's strange, don't you?" I fell back in the bed, tucking a hand behind my head as I watched him take a sip of water. Beautiful lips that were so off-limits. Rolling Adam's apple that exemplified masculinity.

"I think it's a unique situation." He replied.

"Which is a politically correct way of saying it's strange." I sighed when the delicious smelling mask started to tighten as it dried on my face.

"Listen, woman, if I thought it was strange, I'd say that." He placed his water on the nightstand and eased his back against a chocolate leather headboard. "You done any research on it?"

"On what, products of rape seeking connections with their rapist parents? I doubt I'll find anything." I blew out another sigh.

"Wait, you wanna meet this dude? Now *that's* strange." He said without hesitation.

"Hell no, I don't wanna meet him." I snapped. "There's just things about myself that I wanna understand. Things I didn't get from my mama, you know?"

"You mean like your big toe and your second toe being the same length?" He bit into a green apple.

"Really, Chad?"

"What? You volunteered that information. I'm just demonstrating how well I retain things."

"And I'm being serious." I barely smiled, because this had been pressing on my mind and I couldn't imagine anybody more open to discuss it with. Me and my bandmates were as close as siblings, but there was something about Chad that made me feel like I could tell him anything. And I didn't necessarily consider the presence of God absent in my life, but Chad was the first person I'd met this close to my age who'd invited me to pray.

"My bad." He cleared his throat and straightened his handsome face. "Lemme think."

"Think of what?"

"Of what Jesus would do."

"Seriously? This is not a situation that can be resolved by a WWJD bracelet." I fumed. I loved his humor but I didn't need that now.

"I hate to break the news, but pretty much every situation can be resolved by a WWJD bracelet. Also, I think it would benefit you to know that I'm ministering to myself right now too. So, bear with me."

I knew what that meant because he'd said it before. And I also knew that it would take a brief moment of silence before he emerged from his thoughts. I don't know if the Chad I'd been FaceTiming was the same one I'd seen leaving Bottoms with the red boned bitch the night we first met. But if it was, he was living proof that there were two sides to a man.

"Ok, so here's what I'm comin' up with…"

"That quick?" I questioned. "I've been mulling over this for over half a year and you came up with something in two minutes? Wow!"

"Ok, first off, you're twenty-three years old. You don't *mull*." He sliced a hand across his throat and clenched his teeth.

I laughed.

I laughed hard as fuck.

"And second," He cleared his throat to prepare me for a short speech. I swear it was scary how well I knew this dude. We had spent way too much time on the phone. "Both of my parents are personal assistants to our Lord and Savior, so, sometimes the word gets to me faster. In the Tabernacle, this is what we call *favor not being fair*."

"If I wasn't so desperate, I'd end this call right now." I smiled because that's what you did when Chad's face was on your screen. You smiled and tried not to throw your panties.

"Wow. Rude!" He hiked his messy brows, then dived into his message. "There's several Bible passages about forgiveness and embracing things we don't completely understand. But I won't bore you with that."

"Bro, resolve. *Please*!" I rushed him.

"It's coming. Jesus, you're impatient." He sucked his teeth and I thumped the screen. "Let me be clear on this, I don't think you should go anywhere near this dude. Not even while he's behind bars with guards flanking him and shit. But I do think you deserve to have your concerns addressed. And you got access to somebody who can help you with that."

"Who, Kenny? Hell no!"

"Why not? That's his cousin, right?"

"It is. But that's…I don't think he'd be cool with that." I said. "This person hurt the woman he loves. I don't wanna add my shit to the shit they're probably already dealing with as a couple."

"Where'd you learn to be so unselfish?" He asked, rubbing his fingers down his chin.

"What?" I piped.

"Here you are, dealing with what has to be the most devastating news of your life, and you're still worried about somebody else's feelings. That's noble as fuck, Taya."

"It's not *noble,* it's human decency. My mother's almost seven months pregnant. I don't need her *or* her fiancé in the middle of this. I can handle it on my own."

"How?" He sharply quizzed. "How in the world do you plan on handling this by yourself when just ten minutes ago you weren't sure if you should be handling it at all?"

"Easy. I'll talk to his mother." I'd been sitting on that response. "I looked her up on FaceBook. And aside from the questionable potato salad recipe she posted, she seems like a decent person."

"Are you crazy?"

"What? She's following the raisin method."

"Not the damn potato salad. Look, you can't do this. Not alone." He firmly stated as if he was daring me to go through with this plan. And even if he was, he wouldn't be able to stop me. I'd already messaged the lady and made arrangements to meet up.

"So, you comin' with me?" I asked and waited for his eyes to fall out of his head.

But they didn't.

They only slanted to the half-eaten apple on his nightstand before he picked it up, took a bite and said "Send me the deets. I'm 'bout to hit up my family to make funeral arrangements right quick."

"What? Why?" I chuckled.

"'Cause Plus and your mama are gonna kill my black ass for not talking you out of this."

"You couldn't if you tried. Now tell me about your day."

He shook his head as I smiled from ear to ear, knowing I'd found in him a friend indeed.

Ten

"I'm sorry. You going where to do what?"

Of the two of my sisters, Penny was the most God-fearing, which was why I'd called her to share the situation I'd found myself in with Taya. I was out of my element in every kind of way. Spending nights on the phone. Shooting texts throughout the day. Keeping up with her tour schedule just to know what the weather was like around her. I had it bad and I knew it and had no idea what to do next.

Four weeks had passed since we talked about Taya visiting her "grandmother", and in a few hours, I'd be picking her up to head over to the lady's house. I didn't bother trying to talk her out of it, though I thought the whole thing was a bad idea. She was as stubborn as she was beautiful, a thing that I admired and was frustrated by.

"I know it sounds crazy, but—"

"That's because it *is*." Penny nearly yelled into the receiver. "You can't let her do this, Chad. What about her mother? What if this lady is as crazy as her son?"

"Well, I think that's where I come in," I said. "You know, in case she needs back up or something."

"What are you, HPD? You have zero experience and I would hate for you to get caught up in the middle of some celebrity drama because you can't see past a pretty face and a slim waist."

"What?" My nose wrinkled as I placed my cell on the kitchen counter to grab a bottled water from the frig.

"*What* ain't what I said. You and I both know what you're after. I have to admit, though, I've never seen you go to these extremes. Didn't think you really had to."

I could hear the snark in my sister's voice. And typically, I'd let it slide because typically she was right. But it wasn't like that this time. With Taya, everything was different. I mean, I wasn't blind, of course, she was beautiful. But I wasn't coming at her as anything but a friend.

"It ain't like that." I returned after draining half the contents of my water bottle. "We're friends. That's it."

"Really? What kind of friends fall asleep on the phone every night?"

"It's not every night."

"Okay, every *available* night. You know what I mean." She smacked her lips.

"Man, I didn't call you for all this." I snapped. What I needed was advice, validation actually. And Penny was giving me everything but that.

"Oh, I *know* why you're calling." She said. "You're calling because you're in over your head and you want your big sister to tell you what to do. But it's too late for that. You've obviously made a promise and now you have to keep it. Now, what color do you want us to wear to your repass? Because Plus is definitely about to have that long head of yours on a stick."

"Actually, I was calling to tell you that Taya loves your *Blessed Assurance Rejuvenation Mask,* but whatever."

"Oh my God! Does she!?" Her voice went up three octaves.

"Probably, but I'm playin'." I had to burst her bubble. "Tell me why I shouldn't do this and I'll shoot her the text right now." I was desperate. There was no telling what was about to go down.

"I'll do no such thing." I could hear Penny's big eyes rolling. "Mostly because you're an asshole but also because it's the bravest thing I've ever seen you do."

"What, walking into a burning building? 'Cause that's exactly what this feels like."

"No, crazy." She chuckled under the sound of Boogie's voice coming from down the hallway begging for a snack.

"What you're doing right now is putting somebody else's needs before your own." She said. "And not being judgmental in the process. That's big. Absolutely gigantic."

I took a moment to breathe that in. I couldn't remember the last time my sister had told me she was proud of me. Not that she wasn't, she just didn't feel compelled to say it all the time. Penny was stern that way. She had to be moved to say things and when she did, you damn near had to document it.

"I appreciate that sis," I said, trying not to put too much light on the situation out of fear that she'd take it back.

"Good. Now go do whatever it is you're gonna do. And make sure you don't D-I-E because your niece is expecting to see you this weekend."

"Who's gonna die, Mommy?" Boogie's little voice sounded. At four years old she could read, write and spell pretty well. I don't know why Penny thought she could still get over on her with the spell it out game.

"Nobody, baby. I misspelled love." Penny cleared her throat and I huffed out a laugh.

"Chad I gotta go. Your nosey niece is up and hungry. I love you." She kissed the receiver.

"Aight. Love you too. Kiss Boogie for me." I smiled and ended the call to go wait on the sofa for a text from Taya.

I should've called and told him, but I didn't.

I don't know why I'd invited him to come with me in the first place when I knew that this was something that I needed to do by myself.

I pulled up to the house, not far from where I grew up. Gray bricks, wood trim, one-story, short porch. The yard was well kept, edges trimmed shrubbery too. Looked like it would've been the perfect place to visit during the summer if my family was normal like everybody else's.

I'd tried my best to talk Cha Cha out of driving me. But she wasn't easily swayed when it came to my safety. We'd only be in town for a few days then we'd be back on the road. I needed to get this over with for my sanity before my focus started to sway.

Mama wouldn't be joining us on the rest of the tour. Her belly had dropped and under doctor's orders, she was no longer allowed to travel. I wished I could drop everything and stay at home with her. But she'd have Aunt Rhonda with her til we wrapped up the tour. Hopefully, the triplets could hold off until then.

For now, I was on a secret mission to meet someone and my mother would kill me if she knew. Seeing as Cha Cha didn't talk, she was the perfect ally. I'd simply walk in, get what I came for, and go on about my life.

At least that was the plan before I knocked on the solid wooden door and a woman opened it with eyes just like mine. I'd assumed that all my feminine traits came straight from my mother, but there was no denying those high, sharp cheekbones and jet black mane streaked in gray that hung down to her shoulders. If this woman wasn't my grandmother, then I didn't have one.

"Taya?" Her voice was low and heavy, riddled with pain. Such a strange thing to hear.

"*Hmm hmm*, yes." I cleared my throat, having gone over what I'd say a million times on the way over. But in that moment, my mind went blank and all I wanted to do was burst into tears.

"Do you...you wanna come in?" She held the door open with a long arm that sprouted a long hand with even longer fingers just like mine. Smooth brown skin looked worn but still pretty. Like life had tried to kill her and almost succeeded.

"Ye...yes ma'am." I moved forward, pausing to look over my shoulder and make sure Cha Cha wasn't more than a step behind.

"This is my security guard, Cha Cha," I said. "She goes with me everywhere." I offered an awkward smile.

"I understand." She nodded her head, stepping in before me and Cha Cha followed behind her. She secured a chain latch at the top of the door and ushered us into the tiny living room.

The smell of Pine-Sol and mustard greens poured into my senses like Christmas Day. I wondered if her house always smelled like this or if she only woke up these scents for special occasions. There were pictures on all the walls, and I tried not to look too hard out of fear that I might see… *him*.

And then I did.

A fairly small picture compared to all the others. I recognized him from the search I'd conducted on the sex offender registry the minute I found out his full government name.

He was younger in the photo, maybe in his early twenties, wearing a red Chicago Bulls Bomber jacket, two sizes too big. And part of me wished somebody had choked him to death with it. The other part was glad they hadn't because, without him, I wouldn't be here.

"I'm so sorry." She noticed where my eyes had landed and hurried over to the picture and snatched it off the wall, nearly ripping it in half in the process. "I thought I took this down. I'm… I didn't mean for you to have to see that. I can only imagine—"

"It's okay." I calmly stated. "You don't have to be sorry for that. I'm sure this is just as awkward for you as it is for me."

She didn't confirm or deny. Just bowed her head and motioned for Cha Cha and I to take a seat. Cha Cha, of course, opted to stand guard at the door.

"So, would you like something to drink?" She asked. And it must've been close to impossible to keep a straight face with who I was and how I'd come to be and the fact that I was voluntarily sitting in her living room.

"No. I mean… Miss Brenda, I didn't come here for pleasantries." I couldn't sit through a round of bullshit. I literally didn't have time. "And I don't mean to be disrespectful, but I have questions for you. Questions that have to be answered today because I don't plan on ever coming back."

She took a seat on the sofa across from me, placed one hand on top of the other in her lap and said, "Okay. Ask away."

So I did.

I asked if she knew her son was a sexual predator before he raped my mother. And when she said *yes* I asked why she didn't do anything about it.

"I didn't know what to do." Was her response. And that infuriated me to the point that I had to clench my fists to anchor myself.

"I know it sounds stupid." She continued, looking down at my hands then back up at the tension in my face. "But when you're from where I'm from when you've gone through what I went through, it's not as easy as seeing a problem and fixing it. This has been going on in my family since before I was born. I hate to think that it's as simple as this but I truly believe that part of the reason I wound up with Rodney's father was because he saw a victim in me and took advantage."

She stopped to run her tongue along the front of her teeth, eyes glistening and heavy with impending tears. I didn't know what to say, so, I said nothing.

"I know that's no excuse." She kept going after the silence had settled for long enough. "But Rodney did what he saw, which was abuse. And I did what *I* saw, which was nothing." Her voice squeaked and a levee broke in her eyes, sending tears cascading down her cheeks.

"I'm sorry for what happened to your mother." She ran a finger across her running nose. "And anybody else that my son hurt. I really am. I lost my daughter to this and I will never forgive myself. *Ever*." She balled up both her fists and stood from the sofa, walking away from the living room with both hands planted at the trunk of her back.

"I'm sorry, you said… you said you lost your daughter?" I'd seen pictures of a young girl on the wall but never questioned who she was.

"Yes." She cleared her throat, straightening herself as she turned back around and folded her arms across her chest. "Charlie. She was, umm, she was twelve when she…when she died."

"I'm so sorry. Was she sick?"

"No, she… she killed herself." The pain in this woman's voice was so thick it almost completely filled up the room. "Rodney'd been…he hurt her. Had been for years and I didn't protect her like I should have and I guess it just…it got to be too much." Her lips trembled and before long she was crying again.

"Your own daughter?" I couldn't believe what I was hearing. "You let that monster abuse your daughter and you didn't do anything? What is wrong with you?" I was enraged for a child that I didn't even know.

"But you don't understand!" She pressed her hands together as if she were praying.

"What is there to understand? She was your child. Yours to protect against anything and anybody. Even your disgusting ass son."

I'd never taken this tone with an elder, but this was different. The whole story was a mess. My mother had damn near sacrificed her sanity to keep me safe and this woman allowed her child to suffer and ultimately die.

"I know you think I'm a horrible person." She wiped her tears, eyes fixed on me. "But I'm not. I may have been weak, but I'm not a bad person."

"With all due respect, you are *both*." I spat. All that I could think of was a twelve-year-old girl living in so much pain that she would rather be dead.

"If that's how you feel—"

"This ain't about my feelings, it's the truth. Your daughter is dead and I'm here! Here with no hopes of ever forming a relationship with either of my grandparents because one set is dead and the other set is a pair of monsters!"

I screamed, tears rolling down my cheeks, throat burning with raw emotions that felt like fireworks going off inside me. Through the fog of tears, I could see her walking toward me. Was she about try to comfort me? Did she have the fucking nerve?

"Don't touch me!" I pulled away as soon as her hand touched my shoulder.

"I'm sorry, I—"

"No." I raised a palm. "No, you're not sorry. Not sorry enough. You could never be sorry enough. Do you know how many lives have been ruined while you protected your son? How many little girls will grow into broken women because you didn't stand up to him? *If* they live?"

"Yes, I do." She replied, straightening her stance. "In the past year, twenty women have come forward, and I've been at every courtroom preceding testifying on their behalf."

"I'm sorry, what?" My mouth fell open.

"I can't undo it." She said. "I can't bring Charlie back. I can't mend the babies he hurt. But I can be there. I can show my face and tell my side of things and if it means I'll be serving time, then so be it."

She seemed so settled in what she'd just said that it rerouted my thoughts. It pulled the focus off of how negligent she was and placed it somewhere else. I didn't wanna hug her or offer forgiveness because she hadn't asked for it and it wasn't mine to give. But her actions were an example of better late than never. Too many people grow old without seeing the value in that.

"I don't expect to see you here again." She said, walking over to an old radio and pulling a cassette tape from one of two decks. "Didn't expect to ever hear from you at all given the circumstances. But I'm glad you came." She held the tape in her hand like it was a prize possession.

"Why?" I asked, confused.

"Closure." She extended a gray cassette with *'McKinley'* written on it in warn permanent marker.

"Charlie left this for Kenny." She said. "Wanted him to know she didn't blame him for what happened."

"Why would she blame him?" I asked, part of me not even wanting to know.

"It's not my place to tell you." She released the tape and backed away. "He didn't hurt Charlie if that's what you're thinking. They were bosom buddies. He looked out for her as much as he could."

I looked down at the tape then back up into her eyes. I'd never seen a face so sad and worn. What was keeping her here? What motivated her to climb out of bed every morning knowing she'd allowed so much pain to be inflicted on so many lives?

"I don't know if I have the right to ask why you came here today." She swallowed, hands folded together in front of her.

"I um…" I hesitated. I knew why I'd come but wasn't sure I'd gotten it. "I guess I needed closure too."

"Well, I hope you got it. Or something close to it. I wish there was more I could do." She breathed out. "And if it's any consolation, your mother did an amazing job raising you. I don't know too many people who'd put their selves in this position. You're brave. Much braver than I've ever been."

Thank you didn't seem like the appropriate thing to say seeing as courageous was far from how I was feeling. Conflicted. Sick to my stomach. No closer to resolve than I was before I walked through her door. All of a sudden, I understood why Mama didn't want me to know about this. Ignorance would've been more blissful than what I was feeling now.

"I think we're gonna leave." I took a deep breath and exhaled, head spinning with thoughts of what to do next.

"Ok." She nodded, not moving from where she stood as Cha Cha unlocked the door and pulled it open.

I hated the look of hopelessness in Brenda's eyes when I looked back at her over my shoulder. "Are you gonna be okay?" I asked. The human in me wouldn't allow me to leave without at least showing some kind of concern.

"Yeah." She nodded, voice barely above a whisper. And I didn't believe her at all.

With my heartbeat pulsing in my ears and my mouth as dry as a desert, my feet began to move on their own fruition, landing me right in front of this woman. Dismissing all judgment and temporarily voiding her mistakes, I pulled her into a tight hug, her sobs exploding on my shoulder. I couldn't help but do the same. It was like some kind of chain reaction, and though I knew it wasn't likely that we'd see each other again, I couldn't imagine leaving her house without a meaningful exchange. Be it complicated and saturated in pain, it was an experience nonetheless. The same blood that flowed through her veins flowed through mine, and that alone warranted sympathy if nothing else.

Eleven

"Taya—"

"I already went!" She bawled, falling into my chest as soon as I opened the door.

"I'm sorry. I shoulda called you. But I thought I could handle it by myself. And it was bad. It was so, so bad!"

I could hardly make out her words, she was crying so hard. She'd soaked the front of my shirt and I had to pry her off of me to look into her eyes.

"Tell me what happened." I pleaded. "Did somebody hurt you?"

"No." She shook her head, breathing erratically. "Nobody hurt me. It was just so bad. I really messed up. I shouldna went over there, Chad. Now I know why Kenny didn't want me to go. Now I know why he's not really close with his family. It is sickening." The words tumbled out of her mouth. She was a complete mess and I had no idea what to do.

"Come sit down." I grabbed her by the hand and led her over

to the sofa. "It's okay." I pulled her in against my side, roping my arm around her shoulder until I could feel every breath she took.

"I got you," I assured her though I was winging this shit. "Where's Cha Cha?"

"She's outside." I could feel an ease in her breathing, which was a good sign.

Maybe.

I didn't know what the hell I was doing.

"What made you change your mind?" I dropped my head to the side, resting it on top of hers, the sweet scent of her perfume unintentionally intoxicating me.

With her hand nestled in mine, I rubbed my thumb across her palm, warmed at the sight of the tiny dot I'd left on her ring-finger, not surprised that she didn't resist. We literally fit like puzzle pieces.

"I don't know." She breathed out, shoulders expanding against my ribcage. "But I regret it. And not just going alone. I regret going *period*."

"Damn, that bad?"

"Yeah, that bad." She sighed again, nestling her head into my chest. "It was so dark and heavy and sad in that house. And I think she tried to cover it up. She cooked and cleaned up like she was gonna be able to mask all of it. Keep me safe from it or something. But she couldn't. The minute she opened her mouth it was all out. You know?"

I didn't say anything because I *didn't* know. But what I could feel from her body, the literal shift in her spirit, she probably knew too much.

"Are you mad at me?" She looked up at me and asked, magical brown eyes now darkened with sorrow.

I hated that shit.

"No." I lied. I was a little pissed. Maybe if I'd gone with her I could've taken half the blow. If I'd seen what was going on, maybe I could've gotten her outta there before it went as far as it did.

"You thirsty? Hungry? Think I got an expired salad in the frig." I tried changing the mood because the thought of her being anything but happy messed with me.

"I'm not hungry." She attempted to smile, and that was enough to send my stupid heart fluttering. "Especially not for an expired salad." She tipped her head up to look at me again.

"You wanna talk about it?"

"Not really. I mean, I probably need to. But I don't wanna dump all that on you. It's some heavy shit."

"Well, it's a good thing I got these broad ass shoulders." I squeezed her tight and planted a kiss on her forehead.

"Come on, give it to me," I said, literally requesting that the weight of her worries be transferred to me.

By the time Taya finished telling me all that had gone down, she'd drenched the front of my shirt and fell asleep under my arm with her head on my chest. Perfect was the only way to describe the way she felt so close to me. I wished it hadn't been under these circumstances, but there was no place I'd rather be.

The doorbell rang and startled her awake. I slid my arm from around her to go see who it was. One look through the peephole and my heart damn near left my chest. I should've known it wouldn't be long before the troops showed up.

"Preacher Boy, I know you got my baby in there!" The pounding grew louder as the pregnant lady with Taya's cheekbones stood on her tiptoes and pressed her eye to the peephole.

"Shena, calm down, man." I could hear Plus's always calm voice trying to wrangle his old lady. If it weren't for the

seriousness of the situation, I might've busted out laughing.

I unlocked the door, then stepped back to pull it open, looking over my shoulder to find Taya looking at me apologetically. It was what it was at this point. There weren't too many other ways for this to unfold.

"Hey—"

"Where is my daughter?" Tashena didn't even let me finish speaking before she pushed her way in and made a beeline straight to Taya.

Plus looked like he wanted to step in and slow things down, but not even one of the most influential men in the world could stop a mother from getting to her child.

"We know where you were. Have you lost your mind?" Tashena fumed, stopping in front of Taya who was now sitting straight up on the sofa.

"Mama—" Taya tried before Tashena cut her off.

"Mama my ass! Do you have any idea how crazy this is?" Tashena continued with a hand resting on her hip, visibly flustered with the weight of three babies bending her back. "You don't even know that woman. Don't know a damn thing about her and you decided to just up and run over there without asking anybody? What if something had happened? What if she flipped out and—"

"Tashena, sit down." I guess Plus had seen enough and made his way over to help, or should I say force, Tashena down onto the couch.

"Taya, you alright?" He asked his stepdaughter with a calmness that was the complete opposite of his fiancé's demeanor.

"Of course, she's not fine. Look at her eyes." Tashena breathed out, now sitting on the couch next to her daughter, leaning forward as far as she could with a belly in the way, then staring into her eyes. "Did she upset you? Did she put her hands on you? 'Cause if she did, so help me God."

"No." Taya shook her head, eyes blinking closed before she opened them to look at her worried mother. "She didn't hurt me, Mama. And I'm sorry you're upset, but I'm not sorry for taking matters into my own hands."

"What matters?" Tashena squeaked.

"Questions." Taya returned. "Questions that nobody could answer but her. Questions that have been keeping me up at night since the day I found out the truth."

"Taya—"

"I know," Taya said. "It doesn't make sense to you. And I mean no disrespect when I say that it doesn't have to. I needed to talk to her. To look at her in order to look at myself. And it hurt like hell seeing somebody in that much pain. I wanted to hate her or feel anything but this emptiness that just… it just consumes me sometimes. But I couldn't. I don't."

"Baby," She rested a hand on Taya's thigh, temper cooled that quickly as she tried to soothe her daughter.

"Did y'all know other victims have come forward since Bella, and Brenda's been testifying on their behalf?" Taya asked. She'd told me that Bella was a neighbor's kid who'd been molested by Taya's biological father.

"No." Tashena quickly replied.

"Yeah." Plus shoved his hands in his pockets.

"Wait, what? Why didn't you tell me?" Tashena squeaked, looking up at Plus.

"'Cause you're pregnant and you don't need to be worried about that shit."

"But I—"

"He's right, Mama." Taya grabbed her mother's hand. "Think about the babies."

"I *am* thinking about the babies. *You're* my baby."

"And I'm *fine*." Taya's eyes widened as she turned sideways to face her mother. "At least I will be as long as we can keep going to counseling together."

"Oh…okay." Tashena squeezed Taya's hand. "Okay." She blew out a breath and rubbed her belly.

"Kenny, I'm hungry. All this drama worked up my appetite." Tashena said.

"Yeah, mine too." Plus shook his head. "Chad, I owe you for this. Taya, you good?" His eyes slid from me to Taya who was sitting on the sofa watching her mother accept defeat and get up with Plus's assistance.

"Yes." Taya nodded. "And I'm sorry for worrying y'all."

"Umm-hmm." Tashena rolled her eyes, warranting a squeezing of her hand from Plus. "And we're not done." She rolled her eyes, then stopped to give me another once over.

"I know." Taya stood up and gave her mother a tight hug. "I love you." She placed a kiss on her cheek before reaching in her pocket and retrieving what appeared to be a cassette tape.

"Kenny, this is for you." She extended the tape to Plus.

"What's that?" He asked brows scrunched with confusion.

"I didn't listen," Taya replied. "Your aunt said Charlie left it for you."

"Oh my God!" Tashena's hand went to her chest. "Kenny—"

"It's fine." Plus swallowed, looking down his arm at Tashena. "Thank you. Y'all have a good night." He pulled Taya in for a side hug, then released her and ushered himself and Tashena out of the door.

I woke up with his heart beating in my ear after falling asleep under his arm with my head on his chest. I'd powered my phone off because I knew my mama would be blowing it up as soon as Kenny drifted off to sleep, and when I powered it on, my notifications were filled with text messages and missed calls. I opened the first text from my mama and almost fell over the coffee table jumping up off the sofa.

"You alright?" Chad squinted, stretching his arms and sitting up, sleepy eyes fixed on me as I hurried over to the kitchen bar where I'd left my purse.

"Yeah. I mean no." I hurried. "I gotta go. Thanks for everything. I'll call you, okay?" I rushed toward the door.

"What? No." He cleared his throat, standing from the sofa and rubbing a hand down the back of his neck. "Where you goin'?"

"I missed a few calls from my mama. Apparently, her water broke like three hours ago. They're at the hospital. I need to go."

"Okay. Then, I'll take you." He offered, voice groggy in the sexiest kind of way as he rubbed a finger across his eye. "Which hospital?" He brushed past me in route to his bedroom, shirt wrinkled from sleeping in it and me sleeping on him.

"Chad, you don't have to—"

"I know. But I am." He emerged from the room pulling a fresh shirt on over his head. Even in high-pressure situations, this dude found it necessary to be presentable.

"Let's go." He gave me his eyes long enough for me to see that he was serious, concerned, and determined to make me understand that being there for me was something he didn't mind doing.

Just under three weeks before Christmas, I gained one little brother and two little sisters. Weighing in at four pounds and a few ounces apiece, baby boy, Charlie, and his identical twin sisters, Taj and McKinzey, made their grand entrance on December seventh, forever changing the dynamic of our little family. I barely made it to the delivery room in time, despite the fact that Chad was driving like everything but a Christian. But there's no doubt in my mind that my mama controlled even that. There was nothing this woman couldn't do.

After crying our eyes out and thanking God for three healthy babies, I left mama to be alone with Kenny while I walked down to the nursery to look in on the triplets. They were so little. I don't think I'd ever been that close to beings so small. And they already looked like somebody, as Aunt Rhonda would say. Charlie looked like Kenny had spit him out, so pale that you could see his veins through his skin. Mama kept telling me he'd gain some melanin in a few weeks because the Lord wouldn't leave her in charge of raising a light-skinned son. I reminded her that Kenny was only a shade darker than beige, and all she could do was look up at him and roll her eyes while he sat next to her with a grin plastered on his face. The girls were a few shades darker than their brother, with heads full of jet-black curls and round brown eyes that were surprisingly wide open most of the time. They were perfect, for lack of better words. And I knew the moment I sniffed their little necks I was gonna have a hard time going back on the road without them.

"You calculating how many diapers you're gonna have to change?" Chad's voice sounded as he headed toward me from down the hallway. "If so, I can assure you, you ain't ready." He hiked a brow, grinning like a Cheshire cat.

Fine ass.

"Actually, I wasn't even thinking about that." I glanced at the triplets again before returning my eyes to Chad. "You just gave me a reason to get happy about going back on the road." I smiled, shoving my hands in the pockets of my jeans as he stopped and stood beside me.

"Babies are tricky." He looked through the thick glass window at my siblings. "God makes 'em cute on purpose so you'll forget what goes down in those diapers." He shook his head.

"And what do you know about babies?" I asked, watching him as he watched the babies.

"A lot." He breathed out, taking his eyes off the infants to stare at me.

"Oh yeah, *Super Uncle*."

"The one and only!" A sense of pride filled his voice at the mention of little Miss Patience.

"So, being an uncle makes you an expert? I doubt your sister left you alone with her for more than five minutes at a time." I teased, nudging his side with my elbow.

"You'd be surprised." He winked.

"Oh, *would* I?" I widened my eyes.

"You would." He returned, then looked down at his shoes.

After a short pause, he asked, "So, how long before y'all head out?"

"We're actually supposed to be leaving tonight."

"Damn, that soon?"

"Yeah," I said. "Why, you miss me already?" I looked to the side to find his eyes still fixed on his shoes, fighting the urge to blush though I knew him just well enough to know that he wanted to.

"Nah, It's just…your mom just gave birth. I thought y'all might postpone things for a minute."

"Yeah, maybe in a perfect world," I said. "But in *Plus's* world, the show must go on."

I might've sounded discouraged but that wasn't my intention. I totally understood all the sacrifices Kenny'd made to get to where he was in life, and that work ethic didn't stop with the birth of the triplets. If anything, it was amplified. They, along with Oakley Rose, would someday carry on his legacy. And what good would it do his legacy to cancel tour dates to change diapers?

"Yeah. I guess so." Chad returned.

"You sure that's your only concern?" I had to ask. His inability to look me in the eyes was a direct indication of things being withheld.

"It's not, actually." Now he looked up. And the heat from his stare sent my heartbeat into overdrive. Everything about Chad's presence had an effect on my senses and it was all I could do not to confess.

"I don't know if this is the right place to be having this conversation." He continued, eyes squinting, nervous energy traveling from the tips of his fingers.

"What conversation?" I looked down the hall past him, then planted my attention on his beautiful brown lips.

"I miss you." He blurted and I thought I might die. "And I know we talk all the time. I know I'm probably occupying too much of your space already, but I can't help it. I tried." He breathed out a nervous chuckle that made me want to plant both of my hands on the sides of his face and kiss him until he understood that there wasn't a space in or around my body that I wouldn't surrender to him.

But I couldn't do that.

It was too soon, and Chad wasn't the type to stay interested once he got what he came for. Speaking of which, I couldn't even give him *that*. Wouldn't have the slightest idea what to do with all that he was. And he'd definitely run away screaming if he knew the truth. That the pretty little songbird who walked with the confidence of a grown woman was, in fact, still a child in all the ways that mattered.

"Chad, I—"

"I know." He cut me off, rubbing a hand down his face. "My bad. I probably need to get some sleep. You need me to take you home or…"

"No." I cleared my throat. "I'm gonna stay and…you know, stare at the babies. But thanks. Thanks for everything. I really appreciate you being there today. It meant a lot."

"No problem." He looked at me then quickly dropped his eyes to his shoes again. "Tell your mom and Plus I said congratulations."

He hurried off down the hallway before I could say another word and I instantly felt sick to my stomach. What would've been the harm in saying *'I miss you too'*?

Twelve

Five months, twenty-five cities, and forty-five shows after kicking this whole thing off, we were finally back at home and done with *The First Semester Tour*. Kenny had planned a two-week long vacation in the Caribbean for The Crew, but first, we had to get home and get acclimated to life off the road. It was kind of like returning from space in a way. Not rushing to and from press junkets or having our hair and limbs pulled in different directions by stylists and choreographers. I never thought I'd be sitting in my bed thinking this, but I kinda missed the old tour bus.

"Bitch, why my mama tryna come on the trip?" Bre walked into my room like it was her own, head full of bundles under a fuchsia bonnet that matched her fuchsia nails and the fuchsia onesie that had her looking like a chocolate filled Energizer Bunny.

"Why wouldn't she?" I asked, staring at my phone, smiling at all the videos fans were posting from our tour on Instagram and SnapChat. "Kenny said family's welcome. It's just her and your sister, right?"

"Yeah. If she don't try to bring her broke ass boyfriend."

"You mean your stepfather?" I looked up to catch her reaction because I knew how much she hated her mama's boyfriend and wouldn't acknowledge him as anything but that.

"You lucky I couldn't find no Kool-Aid in that empty ass refrigerator or I'd throw it on your ass right now." She came over and flopped down at the foot of my bed, grabbing a cushion from my fury bench and tossing it at me.

"Girl, you know you like Mr. Richard. I don't know why you keep being like that." I giggled and chunked the cushion back at her.

"Mr. Richard is a broke, roaching ass grandfather of twenty who didn't start liking my mama until he saw her youngest daughter on TV. Swear, she's so desperate to have a man she don't even recognize game."

Bre rolled her eyes, and laid back, flipping out her phone and taking a selfie with her lips puckered. I understood too well the dynamics of mother-daughter relationships. But her and her mother had some serious issues. They could barely be in the same room without an argument erupting. And her sister didn't help things. You'd think being five years older than Bre would make her more mature. But that wasn't the case, at least not from what I could see. Whenever she came around there was a sense of jealousy toward Bre that you'd have to be blind not to see. I never heard her say anything positive. No *"I'm proud of you, lil sis."* Or even an *"I love you."* for that matter. Just eye-rolling and impatience like she had better things to do than eat free meals and go on shopping sprees that her ungrateful ass didn't deserve. Bre was way too good to her mother and her sister for them to treat her the way they did. And that's probably why she kept her distance when she could. Honestly, I didn't blame her for not wanting to bring them on the trip. But she needed somebody there that shared the same blood. It was only right.

"So, who're you dragging along?" Bre turned her head to the side after taking a dozen selfies and uploading them to SnapChat without needing a single filter because her skincare regimen was admirable.

"Nobody." I looked up from the corner of my eye at her then responded to a fan who left heart eyes and commented *'Come thru, lips!'* on a candid shot of me on stage during our last show, belting out the hook to a fan favorite, *'Who Is She?'*. "I invited Kanika but she had other plans."

"Good." Bre smacked her lips. No surprise.

"I knew you wouldn't cry about that. Now you can have me all to your jealous self."

"Jealous?" She cut her eyes. "Girl, ain't nobody jealous of your lil toothpick-built friend."

"Then why are you always so mean to her?" I scrolled down and double-tapped a few more comments to make somebody's day.

"Because she's fake," Bre replied. "And you can't see it because you suck at reading people."

"I do not!"

"You do too!" She retorted. "Case and point, Chad."

"What?"

"Don't *what* me, trick. Did you invite him? 'Cause Stevie Wonder can see that he's in love with your ass and I know you ain't tryna be on an island playing with yourself when you can have somebody there doing it for you." She ran her tongue across her lips and tickled the bottom of my foot.

"Girl, stop!" I pulled my foot away from her perverted fingers. "And I haven't talked to Chad since…"

"Since when?" She asked.

"Since the triplets were born."

"Taya!?"

"What?" I shrugged, dropping my phone on the nightstand and slipping my feet under the covers.

"How do you go from talking to somebody every night like a pubescent teen to not talking to them for two months? Did the babies scare you that bad? You *do* know you can't get pregnant over the phone, right?"

"Fuck you!" I spat.

"I'm just sayin'." She threw up a hand. "We all know your mama sheltered you from shit. Gotta make sure." She looked at her phone as notifications started to come thru in response to the snap she'd just uploaded.

"Yeah, she did." I sighed, head falling back against the headboard. "Speaking of which, do you think I'm a goodie two shoes?"

"A goodie *what, what*?" She looked at me like I'd spoken a foreign language.

"You know what the hell I said," I smirked.

"I do. And I also know you're not forty fuckin' seven years old."

"Whatever. Could you just answer the question?"

"Yes." She didn't hesitate.

"Yes, you'll answer the question?" I slanted my eyes down at her as she scrolled through notifications.

"*Yes* is the answer to the question." She replied without looking at me. "And there's nothing wrong with that. It's why Kenny made you the face of The Crew."

"It is not."

"It is too." Now she looked at me with hiked brows. "And you can stop acting like you don't know. You're damn near perfect, out here reppin' for the *Brandy Norwoods* of our generation. Well, before the fake marriage. It's almost a lost art with everybody tryna be me and shit."

"Be *you*? You say that like it's a bad thing. You're dope as fuck." I said and meant that.

"Oh, I know." Bre flashed a cheeky smile. "But young girls need variety. Black women aren't just one thing. We can be wild or conservative. Reserved or not give a fuck. Sexy or discreet. It's all about balance, you know? Me, you and Kimi represent three completely different kinds of women, and you, my beautiful chocolate mold of perfection, tie it all together in a bow that makes the entire crew worth unwrapping."

"I don't know about all that, but I'll take it coming from you." I grinned.

"Good. 'Cause you ain't got no choice." She stuck her tongue out at me and I did the same in return.

"And Sabre and Jock, who are they reppin' for?" I asked, happy that I could finally mention Jock's name without feeling anything but closure because he'd finally let go.

"The niggas, *duh*." Bre rolled her eyes. "And fuck them. All of 'em. Except Brother Fold."

She wasn't giving me a break.

"What's your fixation with Chad?" I asked chills traveling up my spine at the taste, sound, and feel of his name on my tongue.

"My *fixation* is with the two of you becoming a unit." She admitted. This girl really thought she was cupid. "I can't think of a more perfect match. He's like a reformed hoe around you."

"Bre!"

"What? He is." She piped. "He's fine, so I get why he's coming with some *hoe tags*. But the right woman, *whew*. The right woman could sweep them *hoe tags* right on out the door."

"And what makes you think the right woman is *me*?"

"First of all, I don't *think*. I *know*." She corrected me with a long fingernail pointing in my direction. "I have a sixth sense for things like this. Ask my mama."

"Why would I ask your mama? You hate her boyfriend."

"I didn't hook her up with that baldheaded lying mother fucker." She rolled her eyes. "The man she *should've* been with is the mailman who used to make it his business to change up his route so she could get our child support checks early in the day. But *no*. She overlooked Mr. Harris because he was a few inches shorter than her and now he's married to Sherald."

"Who is Sherald?" I don't know why I always let this girl get me caught up in her tales from the hood, but I couldn't help it.

"My mama's ex-best friend." She said with an attitude. "Bitch swooped in and took Mr. Harris off the market as soon as he made Postmaster. Benefits out the *ass*, you hear me? Sherald is forty-five years old with braces. *Braces, bitch!* You know she cashed in on Mr. Harris's dental insurance. I can't stand that hoe."

At this point, I had tears in my eyes from laughing.

"You laughin', but you need to be taking notes." She slanted her eyes at me, sitting up and sliding to the edge of the bed, onesie fitting her like a glove.

"And what notes should I be taking, ma'am?" I cleared my throat.

"I don't know why you're holding back." She said, seriousness in her eyes as well as her tone. "But I love you like a sister. Probably more than my own damn sister. Definitely more than that sneaky bitch you call a best friend. And I don't want you to miss out on your *Mr. Harris* and wind up with a *Richard*."

I waited for a second then decided to take the weight off this conversation because whether Bre knew it or not, I'd been spending way too much time thinking about Chad already.

"You sayin' I need braces?" I hesitantly made eye contact with the crazy girl who always had my best interest at heart and never hesitated to tell me so.

"I'm serious, Tay." She didn't fall into my trap. "Stubborn recognizes stubborn. And whatever it is you're holding on to, whatever's stopping you from running headfirst into that tall, chocolate, sexy, fine, good smelling, baptized, blessed and highly favored—"

"Damn, you act like you want him," I smirked playfully...*kinda.*

The girl had actually closed her eyes halfway through the description.

"Oh, I do." Her eyes popped open as she bit down on her lip.

"Don't play with me, Bre," I warned.

"Calm down, *Queen Indecisive*. A church boy couldn't handle all this. And his brows are too crazy."

"*You* are too crazy! And I think his brows are cute."

"*Cute* and *crazy* are relatively close to each other in the dictionary. I'd take a tweezer to them shits as soon as he fell asleep."

I busted out laughing and picked my phone up off the nightstand to find a text from my mama with a picture of Plus's two-year-old daughter from a previous situation-ship, Oakley Rose, holding Charlie. So cute.

"Anyway, you just proved my point. You like him." Bre mentioned while I replied to Mama's pic with heart eyes and put the phone back down.

"I can like somebody's eyebrows and even their long legs without wanting to profess my love to them." I returned. "I'm doing me right now. Focusing on my career and keeping it moving like a young G is supposed to."

I knew I'd played myself as soon as I said that. Bre hated when I talked like I was from the *hood hood*, as she would call it.

"Oh, so now you a G?" She curled her lips to the side. "You wouldn't last five minutes in my neighborhood with that soft ass voice. I don't know why you wanna be ghetto so bad." I giggled because she got on my damn nerves.

"It'd help me sleep better tonight if you at least called the man." She sighed, standing from my bed and stretching her arms over her head.

"You goin' to bed already? It's only eight o'clock." I asked even though we were both in our pajamas. I thought we'd at least step out for something to eat.

"Girl, I'm tired." She looked back at me, resting her hand on the knob of my bedroom door. "Being this fabulous is draining. But you wouldn't know." She reached a hand out in front of her and grabbed the air, giving me no choice but to lob a pillow at her as she ducked out of the door.

Not even a minute after she left my room, she sent me a text from her room.

Bre: God told me to tell you to call that man.

Me: No he didn't!

Bre: So, you think I'mma lie on God? Is that the typa bitch you think I am? Wow!

I laughed out loud before replying.

Me: Fine. I'll call him.

Bre: Good. And if he don't want you, shoot him my number!

Me: God told me to tell you to stop playing with me!

Bre: LMMFGDAO

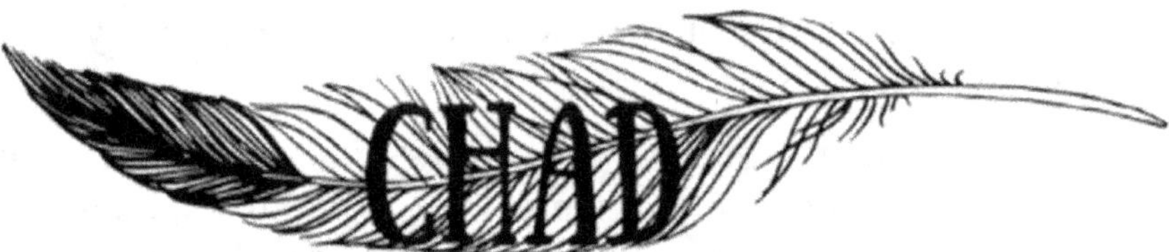

Taya: Wassup, big head?

She'd ghosted me for a minute now she wanted to play.

"Should I even respond to this shit?" I thought to myself.

I shouldn't've been bothered. Wouldn't've been if it was anybody else. But it was her and I was. Even had company coming over to get my mind off it because I didn't think I'd ever hear from her again.

Me: Wassup?

I decided that even though I *was* bothered, she didn't need to know that.

Taya: Nothin'. You busy?

Me: Nah.

Taya: Good. Open the door.

I almost replied "WTF?" but decided to head to the door instead to see if she was playing.

She wasn't.

I looked through the peephole to find her standing there in a red T-shirt with a huge black plus sign on the front and a pair of black joggers that she'd probably been sleeping in before she decided to show up at my door unannounced. Those waist-length braids were pulled up into a knot on top of her head, exposing her long neck and a beautiful face void of make-up, plump lips shiny with lip gloss. I wondered what they tasted like and had to clear my throat and my thoughts before I pulled the door open, blood rushing to my head—both of them mother fuckers—the moment her soft aroma entered the room.

"You sure you're not busy? Smells like something's cooking." She was being way too casual for somebody who'd dropped off the face of my call log, stepping through my door in a pair of sneakers like we were homeboys or some shit.

"It's just nachos." I stepped aside then pulled the door closed as she headed into the living room and made herself at home on the sofa.

"Oh." She looked up at me as I went into the kitchen to turn the burner off on the cheese dip. "I'm surprised you replied to my text."

"Why?"

"You know why." She stood from the sofa having only barely sat back on it in the first place. "I'm sorry." She walked up on me just outside the kitchen. "But when you said what you said to me, I didn't know what to do with it."

"It's nothing." I brushed past her and went into the living room, taking a seat on the sofa and flipping on the TV.

"It's not *nothing*, Chad. And I get why you're being passive, but you don't have to."

"I'm not being anything. Just giving you what you want."

"And what do you think I want?" She was still standing near the kitchen, seemingly hesitant to join me on the couch. And rightfully so.

"Nothing, apparently." I scrolled the *OnDemand* menu for something for me and my company to watch.

"You know what, I shouldna came over here." She sighed, keys jingling in her hands as she headed toward the door. "I won't bother you again. Take care."

"You need to grow up." I shook my head, landing on the first season of *'A Different World.'*

"Maybe that's true." She rested her hand on the doorknob. "But I'm not gonna stand here and talk to somebody who obviously doesn't want me around."

"Whatever, Taya." I blew out a breath and leaned back against the sofa. And just as she began to pull the door open, my company showed up on the other side.

"Taya?" they said. And I didn't need to look up to hear the shock in their voice.

"Hey, Jada!" Taya sounded just as shocked.

"Hey!" Jada pulled Taya into a hug that must've felt awkward for Taya given the current circumstances. "Oh, and this is our sister Angela. Angela this is Tay—"

"I know who she is." Penny wasn't with the fake pleasantries seeing as the whole reason she and Jada had come over was to brighten my spirits, no matter how much I'd begged them not to.

"Nice to meet you," Taya said to Penny, extending for a handshake since my big sis didn't seem open for a hug.

"Um-hmm." Penny shook Taya's hand but didn't shake the judgment she was carrying.

"Ok. Well, I was just leav—"

"Leaving? No. Stay!" Jada cut in. "I don't know if you've heard but my brother makes the best nachos. Come on."

"Thanks, Jada. But I really can't. Y'all have a good night, though." Taya rushed, giving Jada's hand a tight squeeze before darting her eyes in my direction then heading out of the door in lightning speed.

I felt like shit for not stopping her, but I had feelings to protect. I didn't have time for this *ring-around-the-rosy* shit that Taya had going on.

"Um, what the hell did we just walk in on?" Jada's brows hiked, cheeks red as rosebuds as she hung her purse on a hook beside my door.

"Looks like we might've just scared the Devil off," Penny noted, cutting her eyes at me and heading into the kitchen after hanging her purse beside Jada's.

"She's not the Devil." I sighed, getting up off the couch. "Just cryptic as hell."

"Are you just gonna let her leave?" Jada was still standing in the doorway with the door open.

"Why wouldn't I?"

"Umm, because I'm sure she didn't come over here for nothing. Do you know how hard it is for a woman to show her face when she's wrong? There was a time when I would rather have set my lashes on fire than to apologize to Jet."

"Lord, don't we know it." Penny chimed in, pouring tortilla chips onto a plate after washing her hands for damn near three minutes.

"Shut up, Penny. Your evil ass coulda been a little more Christian-like to the girl." Jada rolled her eyes at her sister who was always the slowest to forgive anybody that had wronged her family.

Instead of going back and forth, Penny stuck her tongue out and grabbed a serving spoon to pour meaty nacho cheese over her chips.

"Anyway," Jada smacked her lips, hand propped on her hip. "I'm sure she's still sitting in the parking lot if you're man enough to get over what made you stupid enough to let her walk out the door."

"Man, I'm not runnin' behind no girl. You know that ain't me."

I was just about to drizzle cheese over my own nachos when Angela made her way to the sofa, flopped down with a plate in hand and said, "What also *ain't you* is being so sad over a woman that you prepare comfort food and devour it with your sisters. I hate to say it, bro, but you just might have it bad."

She smacked on her nachos then picked up the remote and pressed play on the first episode of she and Jada's favorite show to force me to watch as a kid.

"Would you look at that?" Jada said joining me in the kitchen. "Me and Penny agreed on something. If that ain't the Lord pointing you in the right direction, I don't know what is."

I took a deep breath and accepted the fact that even if both my sisters were getting on my nerves, there was no denying the pounding in my chest when Taya showed up at my door. I did have it bad. Couldn't stop my mind from being on her every damn day. She had planted herself in front of me and wouldn't move out of the way. I had no choice but to run my lovesick ass down the stairs and at least hear her out.

"Go ahead." Jada had a knack for reading my mind through my facial expressions. "I'll take care of these nachos. We might leave you some."

"I'on't know. Chadwick put his foot in this batch, Jay." Penny yelled from the living room, using my actual name because that's how much she loved me.

"Taya!"

His voice broke through the window like a crowbar and damn near scared me into hitting the gas. I looked up and to the left to find him running out into the parking lot in a pair of sweats and a *PLU* hoodie looking perfect and disheveled.

"Shit!" He was breathing hard, voice muffled because my window was still up. "Could you roll the window down?"

I hit the button and lowered the window because looking at Chad made it impossible to do anything but exactly what he said.

He ran a hand down the back of his head, eyes jotting up to the night sky before they returned to me. "I'm… listen, I don't know what I'm supposed to say, but I'm not sorry 'cause this shit ain't my fault. I shouldna been rude 'cause I wasn't raised like that, but you just… *fuck*, man."

"Step back," I commanded.

"What, you just gon' drive off?" He seemed legitimately pissed, eyes squinting under those majestically messy brows.

"No, I'm gonna get out so you don't strain your neck *not* apologizing."

He wanted to smile. I know he did. But this particular time and this particular set of circumstances didn't call for smiles or any of the other friendly shit that people in love express.

"Good." He breathed. "Almost had a damn asthma attack tryna get out here before you left."

"Should I be flattered?" I pushed the door open and climbed out of the car before closing the door so I could lean against it.

"I can't tell you how to feel, Taya." He sighed deeply before landing his eyes on me. "If I could we wouldn't be standing here right now."

"Try," I suggested. "Try to tell me how to feel. Because I don't know either."

"You know how to feel. You're just scared to do it. And unfortunately, that makes two of us." He professed as I squinted, arms folded across my chest, the intensity of his stare heating my skin.

After a brief pause to gather his thoughts or remember his lines or whatever the hell men who looked, walked, and talked like Chad did, he said "I'm pretty sure you know how I get down. And if you don't, this ain't it. I don't fall asleep on the phone with women and I sure as hell don't chase 'em down in parking lots. But for whatever reason, all of that shit seems like a good idea when it comes to you. And I've tried talking myself out of it. Prayed for answers that would lead me in the opposite direction because God forbid, I give up every woman in the world to play myself for one."

"Play yourself?" I cut in. "Are you serious right now? Is this your idea of winning somebody over? Because if it is, you could use some damn practice."

I stepped forward and turned around to pull at the handle on my door, unable to pull it open before Chad's hand was around my wrist, his body hovering over the back of me like a shadow that wouldn't budge.

"I wasn't finished." He tugged at me gently, giving me no choice but to turn back around to see if the soft command of his voice was being expressed on his handsome face.

And it was.

A twinkle in his eye that signaled pure, unrestrained emotion warmed me completely and all of a sudden, I'd forgotten how to be offended.

"When I told you I missed you, I meant that." He said. "And even though I don't know why you showed up at my door after ignoring me for as long as you did, I can't help being hopeful."

I breathed in and allowed my exhale to skate across his lips in hopes that he'd stand there long enough to let me say all that I needed to say without changing the way he felt.

"You're right. I igged you because I'm scared." I confessed, allowing him to take my hand into his. "I know what you're used to and I'm not... I don't have that experience."

"What?" He squinted.

"You know, the things you do or have done with other women, I can't live up to that. And I wouldn't expect you to settle for lame and boring when you could literally have any girl you want."

"Taya, are you tryna tell me you're a virgin?" He didn't laugh when he asked and that was a good sign, although I didn't know what expression would be fitting.

"I..." I hesitated. Even at twenty-three years old I still struggled to say it out loud. It was nothing to be ashamed of but with every birthday it just felt like sex would never happen. I'd gotten comfortable with it. And it's not like I was saving it for marriage or anything, I just never felt like the time was right. Not even with Jock, and he was literally the object of every girl's fantasy.

But with Chad, that wasn't the case.

Whether it be FaceTime, a text message, or even the thought of him, I could completely imagine giving myself over. And that was scary, dangerously so, seeing as I wouldn't be able to reciprocate the talents of an experienced lovemaker. It seemed like such a silly thing to be concerned with, but being my mother's child, I was always concerned about what I could do for others as opposed to what others could do for me. It was a gift and a curse. A curse that had me pushing away from a man who obviously felt as strongly about me as I did about him. I really needed to get my shit together.

"You don't have to say it. I already know." He damn near shocked my shoestrings untied.

"Wait, you... How?" I stuttered. *Shook* was my new name.

"That's not important."

"Yes, it is. Who have you talked to? Did Bre tell you? I'm gonna kick her ass." I said that last part more to myself than Chad.

"Bre didn't tell me anything." He grinned. "It's just the way you are. I don't just see what you do. I see what you *don't* do too."

"And what do I *not do* that would lead you to that assumption?" My chest rose and fell as I braced myself for what he was about to say next.

"I don't really have an easy explanation." He started. "But I'm mindful of what I'm carrying before I see or speak to you because you carry stuff with you. It's in your smile, your frown, even your diction."

"Like?"

"Like right now, you think I'm crazy." He smiled and he was right. "You think I'm making all this up because how could I possibly know that you look away when something makes you uncomfortable? Or that you twirl a finger through your hair when you're nervous, but only nervous about something good, like talking to me when you haven't all day? When you're nervous about something bad, your voice hikes and you stutter. It's cute but I don't like it. Not unless I'm close enough to fix it. And you don't want me to be close enough, cause that's scary and different and all the things you hide from. You can stop me if I'm wrong."

He was going on and on, dissecting me like an unlucky frog in biology class. And all I could do was stand there and let him, heart pounding in my chest, hanging on his every word. And I didn't bother to retort because he and I knew that everything he said was true. It didn't matter how he knew. Didn't even startle me that he'd paid such close attention to me. I wanted to be defensive. Wanted to scream and fuss and go back and forth about it. But staring into his eyes, tracing the pattern of those thick brows, I was left speechless. Helpless against the presence of a man who was God's and mine by design.

"I'll take that silence as an acknowledgment of the truth." He smirked, and I blinked my eyes closed before opening them on an exhale.

"If you're right, and obviously you are," I said. "What do we do with this? Where do we go from here? Do we fall back into the friend zone? Do we take it slow and see what happens? 'Cause I don't wanna get hurt, Chad. Not by you. Not after you've told me all this."

He didn't give a verbal reply. And honestly, I was glad. Because no words would've been sufficient or tasted as sweet as his lips as he took a single step forward, cupping my face in the warmth of his palms and pulling me toward him with a gentle force that felt like second nature. Slowly and intentionally, he pressed his lips to mine. My eyes fell closed, body desperate to feel him and nothing else. With a calm urgency, Chad swept my lips apart with his tongue, dipping inside my mouth to taste me and allow me to taste him. Up on the tips of my toes I rose because though it was so much more than I'd bargained for, I wanted more and more of this kiss. My breath had gone from warm to hot, blending with his and wrapping around our tongues. I was literally falling where I stood and suddenly understood why this description was given to the descension into love.

As if he could read the direction of my heart, and perhaps my body, Chad lowered his hands from my face and locked them around my waist, holding me there, taking my breath away, painting the inside of my mouth with his tongue. Breathless moans traveled from my throat, caught by his inhale and swallowed like the last supper. I had never wanted so badly something that I was already having. How the hell was I going to find the strength to break away?

"Chad." I tried and failed to speak in a pitch that didn't make it so obvious that I was desperately helpless to the power of his kiss.

"I know." He mumbled into my mouth, sucking my tongue one last time before pulling away and kissing my lips, then my chin, and then the side of my neck.

Every inch of my skin was covered in goosebumps and I doubted I'd be able to move from this spot since my knees were the equivalent of cooked spaghetti noodles. I couldn't believe that all these old lyrics were proving to be true.

SWV must've really gone through this shit.

"I don't wanna leave." My mouth was no longer my own and I said it without thinking.

"Good." He smiled. "Woulda been awkward as hell to watch you drive off after I just gave you the best kiss I had in my mouth."

"Boy!" I punched him in the chest, smiling so hard my cheeks hurt before he squeezed me tight then leaned in and kissed me again. I was floating like a damn feather.

Penny and Jada always overstayed their welcome because I hardly ever invited them over and they wanted to make the most of their visits. Typically, I was the one at their place eating way more than I should, sucking up free A/C and dozing off on their couches. But tonight, they were going all-in with it.

We'd already watched half of season one of 'A Different World' and these busters were still on my couch, telling Taya embarrassing stories and eating up all my damn nachos.

I wished the flying shits on both of 'em.

"Man, it's midnight already?" I stretched my arms for the one-hundredth time since these two weren't getting the hint. Taya looked up at me and smiled from her place under my arm, the sweet smell of vanilla enticing me in ways that I shouldn't have allowed.

"Boy, we see you over there stretching them long ass arms. Penny, you ready?" Jada chunked a balled-up napkin in my direction and rolled her eyes.

"I guess," Penny said. "Since they're sitting on the same side of the room, I guess we can assume our work here is done." Her eyes darted between me and Taya. I shook my head and stood from the sofa to direct them toward the door just in case they changed their minds.

"We're good." Taya stood up beside me, looking directly at Penny who'd taken a while to warm up to her and would probably hold onto those reservations until the day we walked down the aisle.

Walked down the aisle?

I don't think that thought had ever crossed my mind before. And I wasn't planning on getting down on one knee anytime soon, but the fact that I considered it an option was…*God.*

"You better be." Penny returned. "'Cause if you're not—"

"Angela, seriously?" Jada stepped in, grabbing her Tupperware bowl of cheese off the kitchen counter. "Taya don't mind her. She's just old and territorial. Chad, tell her about the *School Bus Protection Agency* when we leave."

"You better damn not!" Penny almost swung on Jada and all I could do was laugh. "Chadwick Fold, if I find out you uttered one word about the *SBPA*, I'm gonna baptize you in hot vegetable oil."

"Now that is the *opposite* of Christian." Jada nudged Penny, gaining a pinch in return before they both rationed hugs to me and Taya then headed out the door, fussing all the way.

"So, what's up with the *School Bus Protection Agency*?" Taya was messy and nosy as hell for not waiting for the door to close all the way before asking.

"Did you just hear her threaten to fry me?" I reminded her. "You're gonna have to use your imagination for that one. I can't risk it." I shrugged, heading into the kitchen to clean up.

"That is so cute." She giggled following behind me.

"What, death threats? You're weird." I turned on the hot tap water, glancing to the side at her.

"No." She bumped my hip, grabbing a plate and placing it in the dishwasher after I'd rinsed it clean. "Your relationship with your sisters. I think it's sweet that they look out for you even though you're a grown man."

I kept on rinsing and she kept on filling the dishwasher without a verbal response from me.

"I'm also sorry that they had to come over tonight." She said. "Especially if it was because of me."

"It's cool." I rinsed the last dish and reached across her to place it in the dishwasher myself. "Everybody gets caught slipping sometimes."

"Is that right?"

"Yeah, it is," I replied. "But I'm not ashamed of it." I dried my hands on one of the chocolate washcloths that Mama had bought me as a housewarming gift.

"And you shouldn't be." She turned around and leaned her behind against the countertop, eyes following my every move as I poured what was left of the nacho cheese into a plastic bowl and placed the pot in the sink, filling it with hot, soapy water.

"Slips turn into falls." The words fell off her lips like lyrics to a song.

I looked up from the sink to find her staring at me in a way that reminded me we were alone, and it was all I could do not to turn the water off and hoist her little ass up off the floor.

But I couldn't handle Taya like that. Not yet. There was too much at stake and I couldn't fuck it up by being aggressive. There had to be a reason or twenty for her to have held out this long, and if she felt the way she said she did about me, it was my responsibility to make it worth the wait.

"So, you wanna…watch some more 'A Different World', or…"

"No." She replied so fast I damn near jumped.

Her eyes had taken on an intense stare. God, I wasn't ready for this.

"Taya, I don't think you're ready for that," I mentioned as her stare grew more intense.

"Ready for what?" Her brows furrowed as she looked up into my eyes, folding her arms across her chest.

"*This*. Me. You're looking at me like—"

"Chad, are you serious?" She smirked. "You think I'm tryna get in your pants right now? Oh my God!" She dropped her arms to the side and dragged into the living room, flopping down on the sofa.

"What? I… it was in your eyes, man." I followed her into the living room and sat down beside her.

"What was in my eyes? Show me." She smiled.

"I'on't know. You were all intense and shit. Like," I gave a silly attempt at mocking her eyes and she busted out laughing because I probably looked like a fool.

"You are so freakin' cute." She giggled, shaking her head then turning sideways and grabbing both of my hands. "I was staring because I couldn't figure out how to ask you to come to the Caribbean with me in a couple of months."

I swallowed. "The what?"

"The Caribbean." She replied. "Plus is taking The Crew on a trip and we're allowed to bring someone along. I understand if it's too much too soon."

"No. No, it's not." I said. "I just need to settle some things at the shop. But yeah, I'm… I'm flattered. I'd love to go. Thank you."

"Cool." She smiled and my chest tightened. All the things I could do to this woman if I wasn't so dead set on not messing this up.

"So, it's late." She took a deep breath, squeezing my hands before letting them go.

"Yeah, it is." I nodded, pulling her hands back into mine, staring into her eyes and giving her no choice but to stare into mine. "I'm glad you came here tonight. I missed you."

I watched her chest rise and fall, pretty brown eyes glistening as she looked at me and said, "I missed you too." Before meeting me halfway, surrendering to the sweetest kiss.

Thirteen

"I hope you packed extra diapers for Charlie 'cause he pooped again, and I just changed him thirty minutes ago!" Mama yelled down the hall at Kenny from the nursery on the first floor.

The mansion we were staying in looked more like a daycare than a vacation spot with the triplets and all their baby furniture occupying the grand room. Oakley Rose was following me around like a little shadow while Baby Seth, my Mama's best friend's eight-month-old son, was perched on my hip, excited about the breakfast we were about to go eat. Kenny had pulled out all the stops, hiring a chef to cater to our every need for the two weeks we'd be staying in the Caribbean. But Mama had refused his offer to hire a nanny because she didn't trust anybody with her babies. I'd never even gone to daycare myself. Tashena Maxey didn't play when it came to her offspring.

Luckily, we did have Aunt Rhonda on board and you couldn't pay her to let those babies out of her sight. She was already at the breakfast table with two-thirds of the triplets when I walked in with Oakley Rose and Baby Seth. My four-month-old baby sisters, Taj and McKinzey, respectfully known as Mac, were strapped into car seats that were nestled into docking stations, babbling in their signature language that sounded like a three-part harmony when Charlie joined in. Of course, he was upstairs getting his little butt wiped *again* since of the three of them, Charlie ate and shitted the most.

"Well good morning!" Aunt Rhonda hurried over to help me with Oakley Rose and Baby Seth, planting kisses on both of their cheeks before we put them in their highchairs.

"Good morning, Auntie." I pecked her on the cheek, taking a seat beside her at the grand breakfast table. "It smells good in here." I took a deep breath, handing Oakley Rose a coloring sheet and crayons that the cooking staff had left at the center of the table just for hcr.

"Don't it?" Aunt Rhonda said. "I tried to get in there to help and Chef Roland almost swatted my hand. Kenny must be paying them good." She giggled and so did I.

"You mean to tell me you don't have enough work with *Baby Central* over here?" I panned my eyes over the little people at the table behaving surprisingly well with their rattles and teething rings keeping up the background noise.

"Girl, I could do this in my sleep." She said with confidence. "As long as I got somebody nearby to change Charlie's little shitty booty every five minutes, I'm good." We both laughed.

"So, when's this lil boyfriend of yours supposed to be showing up?" I was surprised that question hadn't come up sooner. We'd arrived the night before and I hadn't heard from Chad yet. We flew over on Kenny's plane, but Chad wasn't able to make the flight due to conflict with his schedule. I hoped he wasn't flaking on me. We'd been doing pretty good for the weeks leading up to the trip even though our time together was limited due to his workload.

"Soon, hopefully," I replied, picking Baby Seth's toy up off the floor and handing it to him. "I haven't heard from him since yesterday. He was supposed to be catching a flight last night."

"You don't think he backed out, do you? Being around all this family can be a lot of pressure. Hell, your mother alone could scare off a bear."

I mulled it over in my head and concluded that that couldn't be the case. Chad wasn't like that. Family was his thing and he'd survived the worst of my mama's grueling interviews in the weeks leading up to this trip. Even got a little closer to Kenny who admitted out loud that no man would be good enough for me in his eyes, but Chad got points for effort.

"I don't think so," I said as the rest of the group could be heard heading toward the kitchen. "Probably just a delayed flight or something."

"I hope so." She winked at me, then looked up at the gang of hungry negroes entering the dining room.

Sabre had brought his mother, Tina, who looked more like his sister with smooth brown skin, long jet-black locks hanging down her back, and rich brown eyes just like her son's. I could see where Sabre got his calm demeanor. In the presence of so many different personalities, Tina had a calming energy about her that was so quiet yet so effective.

Kimi brought the only member of her family that was willing to attend the trip, her twin brother, Keno, who was a foot taller than her with striking Indigenous features that could easily grace the cover of a billboard in Time Square. He was the opposite of Kimi in almost every way. Where Kimi was sociable and confident, her brother was withdrawn and unsure. It was almost as if the person we all saw wasn't the same one he saw in the mirror. Made me even more curious about Kimi's upbringing.

Jock rolled solo, which was no surprise. He and his folks were pretty distant for reasons that he'd shared with me in confidence. Reasons that broke my heart to think about. He was, however, expecting a guest to fly in. When I or anybody else asked who it was, he was hesitant to respond. Even seemed nervous in my opinion, which was pretty strange for the braggadocios heart-throb that was never scared to flaunt anything. But whatever. His company was his business. We'd all see who it was when they arrived and hopefully, it wasn't somebody else's girlfriend because Jock was not above messing with other people's property.

Lastly, there was Bre who'd finally decided to bring her mother and sister along. She did, however, refuse to pay for her stepfather's ticket, because she hated him with every fiber of her being. Somehow, Kenny got wind of the situation and that Bre's mother was refusing to come if she couldn't bring Richard. Being the big-hearted giver that he was, Kenny agreed to pay Richard's way to pacify Bre's mother, and the rest was dysfunctional history. That group alone was gonna make the trip worth it because a fight was bound to break out and I'd be right there to watch it.

Seth and Phalin were along as Mama and Kenny's guests, rightfully so since they were their best friends. The two of them were the last to make it to the dining room because, in Mama's words, they were probably ducked off in a closet somewhere being *nasty*. I washed those thoughts down with a glass of orange juice and couldn't make eye contact with either of them for the duration of breakfast.

Just as we settled in, the house manager stepped in to let Kenny know there was someone at the door. Kenny wiped his lips then stood up and followed the brown-skinned gent who was as tall as him and a few pounds heavier, leaving everybody at the table on hush, curious to see who'd shown up.

I was happier than my smile could portray when Kenny walked back into the dining room alongside Chad. But my smile morphed into confusion when my friend, Kanika, trailed in behind them. I'd invited her to come almost as soon as Kenny announced the trip, but she'd told me she couldn't make it due to a prior engagement. I found it strange since Kanika had never passed on an opportunity to be around all the celebs I had access to. But now I was thinking maybe she just wanted to surprise me.

"Well, that was nice." I thought.

"Hey!" I stood from my seat and went over to give them both hugs, starting with Kanika and ending with Chad because God knew I wanted to hug him a little longer. "I'm so glad you came. Did y'all wind up on the same flight?"

"Yeah," Chad replied before Kanika, holding onto my hand and leaning in to kiss my cheek.

"Taya!" Bre left her seat and hurried over to me. *"We need to talk right now!"* She grabbed my arm, dragging me away from Chad and out into the foyer, leaving him standing there looking confused.

"What the hell, Bre?" We finally came to a stop at the bottom of the stairs. "What's going on?"

"She ain't here for you." Bre looked over my shoulder toward the kitchen.

"Who? What are you talking about?"

"Kanika, girl. She ain't here for you." She repeated, still whispering.

"What the... what do you—"

"She's here for Jock, Bitch!" She blurted, no longer whispering as she threw her hands up. "I thought that was her li'l mosquito ass face on Jock's screen this morning, but I wasn't sure until now. This bitch here..."

"Bre, are you serious? I know you hate the girl, but damn."

"You're right, I do hate the bitch. But even *I* wouldn't lie on a nigga's dick. And Jock's dick has either been inside your friend or will be soon. He flew that bitch out here, Taya. Right in front of your face. So, which one you want me to slap first?" Bre was cracking her knuckles and securing her bonnet, ready as hell to fight in a mansion in the damn Caribbean.

"Neither." I blew out a breath, shaking my head at this girl. "Even though that hug was loose as fuck and you're probably right. What can I do? They're both grown. They're both single. I can't tell them who to be with."

"You know what, I thought my mama was simple." She said.

"Bre, the last thing I need is you attacking my judgment. We're on vacation. I don't need this shit right now."

"What you *don't* need is your alleged BFF prancing her ass in here like everything is cool."

"But everything *is* cool," I stressed. As upset as I was on the inside, didn't wanna drag Chad or my family through yet another round of drama.

"Whatever." She threw up a hand. "I'm goin' in here to eat my bacon. Sometimes I wonder if our mamas switched babies. 'Cause ain't no way Miss Tashena birthed a punk ass bitch."

"No. What she birthed is a woman who knows when to act a fool and when not to." I bucked my eyes at Bre. I knew she had my best intentions at heart, but our way of handling things just weren't the same.

"Thank you for telling me," I said, linking an arm through hers so she knew I wasn't upset and actually believed her. "And don't worry, I'll handle this. I'll handle *her*. Jock is just being Jock and I'm not wasting another ounce of energy on that project."

"Whatever you say, ma'am." She said, leading us toward the dining room. "But if you tryna get buck, I got a blade and some Vaseline in my purse."

"Are you serious*!*?"

Bre and Taya came back into the dining room looking different, and I tried to act surprised, but it was apparent from how close Kanika and Jock were sitting that they were the subject of Taya and Bre's discussion.

"I wish I wasn't." Taya shook her head, pulling her chair up, eyes darting across the table at Kanika who was avoiding eye contact.

"But it's all good." She looked at me and said. "Sometimes the universe shows us what we need to get rid of when we wouldn't do so otherwise."

"That's…that's big." I cleared my throat, passing Taya the

dish of bacon that Bre had passed to me, after dropping a few slices on my plate.

"I know." She smiled, leaning to the side to plant a kiss on my cheek. "Now, let's eat."

"You sure?" I planted a hand on her thigh under the table. "You got a reason to be pissed. She coulda talked to you about this."

"You're right, she could have." She blinked, glancing at Kanika before returning her eyes to me. "But she didn't. And as trifling as that makes her, I gotta be the bigger person. Besides, I have you here and that's all that matters. So, are you hungry?"

"Starving." I grinned, squeezing her thigh. "But make no mistake, if you need me to have your back on this…"

"All I need is for your lips to taste good every time you kiss me. Can you do that?" She smiled at me flirtatiously, long lashes sweeping up into the air.

"All damn day," I replied, rubbing her thigh one more time before digging   into   my   breakfast

Fourteen

"So, y'all ain't gon' put her out?" Bre wasn't expected to be the voice of reason in this situation since she claimed to smell jealousy every time Kanika stepped into a room.

"Bre, we can't put the child out on an unfamiliar island." Mama chimed in with Mac passed out in one arm and Taj passed out in the other. Charlie, of course, was having his diaper changed by Aunt Rhonda while all the ladies, minus Kanika, sat around the living room falling into a discussion that I wasn't sure I wanted to have.

"I'on't see why not." Bre's sister, Margo, added her two cents. And I couldn't believe she and her sister had agreed on something for once. "She's trifling. I mean I know the boy's fine, but you don't fuck behind ya homegirl. That goes against all the codes."

"Watch your mouth, Margo." Their mother, Patricia snapped, taking a sip from a black tumbler that was no doubt filled with Crown and Coke.

"Where you think I got this mouth from?" Margo rolled her eyes at her mother. Bravest shit I'd ever seen.

"I don't know where you got it, but I know where you gon' find it if you keep playing with me." Patricia sat straight up in her lounge chair, and Bre almost spit out her Margarita laughing at the whole exchange.

"Anyway," Aunt Phalin said, sweeping her eyes over the ladies before landing them on me. "I think the best way to get to the bottom of this is to go talk to Kanika. Yeah, it looks bad. But everything's not always black and white. Sometimes shit can be gray."

"Gray my ass." Now Mama'd sat up. Well, as much as she could with two sleeping babies in her arms. "I'm not saying we should throw the girl out the house but I'm also not saying we should overlook the fact that she just took trifling to a whole 'nother level. It's one thing to, as Margo so eloquently put it, *fuck behind ya friend*. But it's a whole other thing to traipse up in here without even having a conversation about it. That's inconsiderate as fuck."

"Shole is." Bre took another sip from her drink. "And a fight would come with it if I was in your shoes."

"But you're *not*." I sighed. "And thanks for all the advice, but neither are y'all. I came here to have a good time with my family and now I gotta sit down with my best friend—"

"You need to amend that title, sis." Bre cut in.

"Probably." I blinked, then rolled my eyes. "I still gotta talk to her, though. Whoever she is now."

"No damn body." Bre blurted.

"Bre, seriously?" I slanted my eyes at her.

"What? I told you the girl was a snake the first time I saw her. It ain't my fault it took a trip to the Caribbean to figure it out."

"Bre has a point. The girl always did have a sneaky side, Taya." Now, Aunt Rhonda had words.

"Where was all this suspicion when me and Kanika were braiding each other's hair, or going to the mall, or singing into brushes like we were gonna be the next Destiny's Child?" I asked, panning the set of women who'd become psychic all of a sudden.

"Baby, I'm sorry." Aunt Rhonda said, laying Charlie over her shoulder and patting his back. "But you can't just tell a child that their friend might be a rotten apple without breaking their heart. I figured you'd be smart enough to figure that out when you were older."

"So, this was another ploy to protect me from the worries of the world? You and Mama are zero for two right now." I smirked.

"Excuse me?" Mama piped. "I know you ain't tryna blame this girl's *triflingness* on me?"

"Triflingness? Shena, you know that ain't a word." Auntie Phalin said, and everybody giggled.

"Well, it should be." Mama smacked her lips. "And if it's anybody's fault, it's your own."

"How so?" I squeaked.

"This life ain't for everybody, Taya," Mama replied. "You brought the girl into your world, parading Jock around like a red-nosed pit and expected her to be ok with being an audience member. Everybody ain't built like you. Temptation is real and it's especially difficult when you already have jealousy in your heart."

"Jealousy? Kanika's not jealous of me." I returned.

"To the naked eye, it wouldn't seem that way," Mama said. "But how many times has she said she wished she had your life? Not even just the celebrity status. I can remember Kanika going on and on about how lucky you were to have me and Aunt Rhonda looking after you and loving you the way we did. Her saying stuff like that was part of the reason we never pushed her away. But then you grew up and she was still saying it. And as an adult, that's not healthy."

"So, what are you saying? You think she has mental issues or something?" I asked.

"No. I'm not saying that at all," Mama replied. "What I'm saying is that you can't be friends with somebody who wants to *be* you. It's not healthy for either one of you and today is a testament to that truth."

I absorbed the truth of what my mother'd just said, but still had questions to weigh before I said a word to Kanika.

"So, what's Jock's responsibility in all of this?" Margo asked. "He's just as wrong as ole girl if you ask me."

"But nobody *did* ask you, did they, Margo?" Bre darted her eyes at her sister. "Jock don't owe her nothin'. And niggas come a dime a dozen. When she dropped him, she severed ties. Point blank, period."

"This kind of advice is the main reason you don't have a man." Margo couldn't let the moment pass without taking the opportunity to insult her sister.

"The main reason I don't have a man, *Mar-hoe*, is because I don't want one." Bre cut her eyes at her sister who looked more like her than I remembered now that Bre's face wasn't covered in make-up.

"Alright, that's enough, now." Patricia stepped in, but only because Bre was probably about to get the best of Margo.

"You know what, I think we've all had enough for today." Mama looked over at me, dipping her head to motion for me to grab one of the twins.

"Yeah, we have." Aunt Rhonda stood from her seat, rubbing her hand over Oakley Rose who'd been asleep on a fluffy ottoman for the duration of our discussion. "Come on, baby." She said as Oakley Rose blinked her little eyes open and slid off the ottoman to grab ahold of my hand and follow us into the house.

"Taya, can I... can we talk?" I'd almost made it up to the room I was sharing with Bre when Kanika cut me off at the bottom of the steps, eyes glossed like she'd been crying.

"Yeah." I dryly replied, shoulders rising and falling as I breathed in and out. We walked over to the sitting room just beyond the foyer and stood there, each waiting for the other to speak.

"This place is nice."

"Nika, we can skip the small talk." I snapped. I'd already let her make it for a whole day. She wasn't about to soften the harshness of this whole situation with small talk. "Why didn't you say something?"

"What was I supposed to say?"

"That you were seeing my ex and planned on coming on this trip with him. Is that a hard sentence to formulate?"

"It's not that simple."

"And why the hell not?" I'd raised my voice.

"Listen, I don't want Jock and couldn't care less who he's sleeping with. But you're my friend, Kanika. Been knowing me since I was ten. I just expected more, is all. If you wanted the dude, you coulda just said that."

"Everything must seem so easy to you." She said, eyes down on her feet before slowly lifting to stare into mine. "You always got what you wanted. The nicest clothes, all the attention. You were literally smothered with love all your fucking life. And all I could do was catch the spill then go back home to absolutely nothing."

She stopped to catch her breath and run a finger under her eyes to catch the tears before they fell, and I didn't know what to do. Kanika was known for her theatrics. Could literally cry at the drop of a dime. And I always fell for the shit like a dummy, but that wasn't about to happen tonight.

"Am I supposed to feel guilty?" I asked a simple question, knowing she wouldn't have a simple answer. "Do you know how many times I've shrunk to make you feel bigger, Kanika? How many auditions I've passed on because they only wanted me and not my best friend who played piano? No, you don't 'cause I didn't throw it in your face. So, excuse me if I'm bothered about the shit you pulled tonight."

I wanted to walk away.

Had every intention of doing just that.

But as she stood there with tears sliding down her cheeks, something in me felt that wasn't the right thing to do. So, I did what I'd always done and stayed to hear her out.

"I don't expect you to forgive me." She sniffled, nose as red as Rudolph's. "But I'm sorry about all of this. I swear, I am."

"You wouldn't have to be sorry if you didn't do it."

"You don't think I know that?"

"It doesn't seem like it," I said. "You turned down my invitation and took his without saying shit."

"Yes. And I know it looks bad, but contrary to what everybody in this house probably believes, it wasn't my intention to fall for him. And you can't put all the blame on me. Jock is just as wrong as I am."

"Oh really?"

"Yes, really. Who do you think paid for my ticket? Who do you think has been blowing up my phone for the past month going on and on about how much he wants to be with me? You think I was in this alone? It takes two, Taya. He wanted me just as bad as I wanted him."

"You know what's crazy?" I folded my arms across my chest. "You just said all that and still don't realize how wrong you are. Jock's not obligated to tell me *shit* about *shit*. He's not my best friend. Wouldn't even be in my life if it wasn't for the music. But you, you were in my life before all this. You know things about me that no one else does. You've seen a side of me that none of my bandmates have ever seen. But you don't value that. You don't give a fuck about me and probably never did because all you've ever wanted was to be me. And *that's* what this is all about."

"*Be you?*" She smirked, tilting her head to the side sending a long ponytail swinging. "You've really gotten fulla yourself. And obviously being *you* wasn't good enough or Jock wouldna came running behind me."

"Wow!" My eyes went wide, unfolding my arms and dropping them to the side.

"Truth hurts don't it?" She rolled her eyes then grinned at me having no idea how close I was to risking it all to take one step forward and swing on her ass.

"Actually, it doesn't," I spoke instead. "Especially since the truth is Jock only brought you out here because he knew Chad was coming and apparently, he's childish enough to think dating other people is a fucking competition. He only wants one thing from you, Kanika; assuming he didn't already get it. And as for your all-expense-paid trip to the Caribbean? Jock didn't spend a dime. You can thank Kenny for that. But not in person because you and I both know my mama's not as reserved as I am."

"Excuse me?" She propped a hand on her narrow hip, eyes zoomed in on me like a hawk.

"As a friend or *ex*-friend, I'm suggesting that you be careful what you give to a man who has no intentions of cherishing you. I loved you like a sister and you shitted on that. I hope he makes you cum hard enough to get over what you've lost."

I watched but didn't enjoy seeing her face fall on the floor. I only believed that Kanika had the potential to be a good person because my mama taught me that everybody did. Be that as it may, we couldn't be friends. Not after this level of betrayal and certainly not after I'd realized one thing to be true. You cannot be friends with somebody who wants to be you. Imitation isn't always the best form of flattery.

Fifteen

The first week in the Caribbean was level-ten awkward. There was palpable tension at the dinner table for five whole nights before Kanika finally decided it was enough and started eating all three meals in a room she shared with Sabre's mom, Tina. Jock didn't show any compassion after allegedly fucking her in the jacuzzi the first night. Dude was taking the Rockstar lifestyle shit as far as his arms could reach, hitting on one of the housekeepers right in front of the girl's face. And for obvious reasons, nobody felt sympathetic. She'd brought the whole thing on herself.

On the bright side, Jock's behavior eased any suspicions I had of Taya still checking for him. There was no way that we could both be her type.

At least not the recent version of me.

We'd arrived at the end of week two and had experienced the island from land and sea. Plus didn't come up short when entertaining family and friends. Dude spared no expense when it came to having a good time. As cool as that was, there was still more to do. Me and Taya hadn't had time to be alone since the trip was family-oriented, and I got that, but still.

I sent a letter up to her room with one of the maids, praying Bre wouldn't get to it first and tease me about it later. With Plus's help, I'd arranged for us to have an intimate dinner at a quiet spot along the sea. Just the two of us with no distractions and no outside noise to drown us out.

And she obliged.

Sent a similar letter back to my room, in keeping with the style of communication that I'd initiated. It would've been easy to shoot a text. But where was the romance in that? Things were so different with Taya that I'd decided I needed to treat her *differently*.

She appeared at the top of the steps while I stood at the bottom with my hands shoved in the pockets of my slacks, sweating for no reason. She was beautiful, waist-length braids pulled over her shoulder, tight red dress stopping just above her knees with slithers of her chocolate skin showing above and below the navel. My mouth watered at the thought of how sweet her kisses tasted. I had to shake my head and blink myself back into consciousness as she descended the staircase.

"Is she glowing or is this my imagination?" I asked myself.

Was this what it felt like to be in love?

"This is so corny!" Her smile was easily the most infectious one I'd ever seen.

"What? You don't like my blazer?" I tried not to smile too hard. But I seriously couldn't help it.

"I love your blazer, Chad." The sound of her heels clicking against the hardwood floors came to a halt as she stopped in front of me and ran her hands down my collar, straightening me though I knew damn well there was nothing about me that needed straightening. "I also like that we're both rockin' red. I wonder if they got a *Glamour Shot* studio open around here." She tugged at my collar and pulled my lips against hers, igniting a fire in my groin that would not be easily extinguished.

"Mm-hm." Though there were no words, I knew without looking that the throat being cleared was Tashena's because she'd been lurking all week. It was like an alarm went off in her head whenever mine and her daughter's lips made contact. "Y'all look nice. What's the occasion?"

"A date." Plus stepped up behind her and roped his arms around her waist, planting a kiss on her neck that seemed to soothe her enough to soften the stare she'd planted on me. "Now come on and mind your business before the trio wakes up."

"But I was—"

"Have fun y'all!" Plus shouted on his way out of the foyer after picking Tashena up and draping her over his shoulder like a sack of potatoes.

"Oh, they bout to have a good time." I rubbed my beard and grinned, the noise of Tashena giggling and fussing echoing off the walls of the hallway that led to their room.

"You want me to throw up on this dress?" Taya looked disgusted. I smiled and linked an arm through hers then we headed out to the car.

Me: I think I'm gonna do it.

Bre: Do what? Fuck? Tonight? TAYA!!!

Me: What? You think I should wait? I'm so ready I could burst right now!

Bre: Hell nah, you shouldn't wait! Do you know where I got my cherry popped? In the back of my grandpa's Astrovan like a regular hoe from the slums. You better give that man your pearl in the Caribbean, bitch. Ain't no downgrading from that!

Me: LMMFGDAO. Swear to God, I love you!

Bre: As you should. Now stop texting and go hula-hoop on that dick. I'mma need all the deets in the morning…if he don't fuck you to death…

Me: Bye, Bre!

"Hey, you ready?" Chad's voice caught me off guard while I was still smiling at Bre's text. I'd barely touched the food on my plate anticipating what I had planned for the night.

"Yeah, I'm…yeah." I nervously replied, taken aback by his stature.

Damn, Chad was fine.

"Why you smilin' so hard? That champagne kicked in?" He came around to my side of the table-for-two and helped me out of my chair.

"No. I was just texting Bre's crazy behind." I stood and brushed against him, the scent of his cologne woke up the butterflies in my belly. "Hey, would you be okay with not going straight back to the house?" I asked, praying to God he'd agree.

"Yeah, I'm game. What you tryna do, hit a club or something?" He grabbed my clutch off the table and handed it to me. Chad was so attentive. Always a step ahead. It was obvious he'd been raised in a house full of women.

"Actually, I was thinking something more private." I took the clutch from his hand, looking up to the side at him as he held my hand and led me to the front of the restaurant. Cha Cha was there to meet us and ushered us to the truck, closing the door behind us after we'd both climbed in.

"You wanna tell me what's going on here or do I have to keep guessing?" Chad asked, sitting dangerously close to me in the backseat of the Escalade Cha Cha'd been driving us around in for the past two weeks.

"I…I um… I kinda reserved a room for us."

"A what?"

"A room," I repeated, planting my hand on his lap. "I just wanna be alone with you, if that's okay."

"Yeah. You good. But do your folks know about this?"

"Why would they need to know? I'm grown."

"I know. And I didn't mean it like that. I just don't want your mama putting out an APB. I'm not exactly her favorite person."

"That is not true!" I giggled. "And I've already sent her a text letting her know I'll be out late. So, stop worrying. You're like a father hen or something."

"Father hen? So now we just makin' up shit?"

"Shut up!" I chuckled, digging my fist into his chest, showing no resistance when he leaned in to kiss me, leaving the sweet, minty taste of his lips on mine to savor until I could have more.

"You don't have to wait out here, Cha Cha. I'll call you when we're ready to be picked up."

Cha Cha nodded and I must've looked confused as hell, standing at the receptionist's desk wondering what Taya had up her sleeve.

"Oh my God, you're Taya Maxey!" The receptionist squealed, voice void of the accents we'd grown accustom to on the island, trying and failing to keep her composure at the sight of a celebrity standing at her desk.

"Actually, I'm Whitley Gilbert," Taya replied with a straight face, pulling a black card and a note from her clutch and sliding it across the desk.

"Oh." The receptionist's eyes ballooned. "And you are?" She looked up at me.

"Umm, Dwayne Wayne...*I guess*?" I replied, sliding my eyes from her to Taya who was still holding a straight face while I was struggling not to bust out laughing.

"Ok." The receptionist smiled with pursed lips. "Here's your room key. Do you need us to take up your luggage?"

"No," Taya replied sharply. "We won't be needing clothes."

She cut her eyes at me, sliding the card off the counter and sashaying toward the elevator shaft.

I nodded at the receptionist who was all but drooling as her eyes roved from the tips of my toes to the highest lock on my head. I couldn't tell who'd worked her up more, me or Taya. But whatever the case, I had a much bigger fish to fry.

"Where's the fire?" I caught up with Taya just as the elevator doors were opening. She didn't seem nervous, but she was definitely in a hurry.

"You really want me to answer that?" She looked back over her shoulder, lips spreading into a sexy grin that made my mouth water.

"I think you just did." I roped an arm around her waist, pulling her in against me as the doors closed, admiring our reflections in the mirrored wall to the left.

The island sun had kissed her skin from all the perfect angles. Bronzed shoulders glowed against the crimson fabric that hugged her frame like a glove, complimenting the twinkle in her eyes that I unashamedly took credit for. Strumming the small of her back, I nibbled her bottom lip, tasting her and teasing her, encouraging her to inch closer to me as if she wasn't close enough already.

"Taya?" I whispered against her lips, heat from her name leaving my mouth and swirling in the space between our lips.

"Yeah?" She breathed, body completely molded to me, so close that I could feel her nipples hardening against my chest.

"Are you sure?" I asked a question that needed to be answered before we left this elevator. Before we entered this room. Before there was nothing in the world I could do to resist her and these very aggressive advances.

She tipped her chin up, bottom lip slipping free from the captivity of my teeth and simply said, "Yes."

The elevator doors couldn't've opened soon enough as I took her at her word and prepared to have her and let her have me. Effortlessly, I swooped her up in my arms, chocolate legs dangling over the bend of my forearm as I swallowed her up into a kiss that would render both of us unable to breathe. She felt, tasted, and looked like everything I'd ever need. I don't even think she fully understood the hold she had on me. And if she didn't, I wouldn't have a problem telling her.

Ours was apparently the only room on this floor since the elevator opened into a penthouse suite. I was both excited and worried about the place that I'd make love to Taya for the first time. It meant I'd have a standard to live up to and this spot was bigger than my damned apartment.

"What's wrong?" She must've sensed my thoughts, rubbing a hand down the back of my head as I ushered us into a spacious living room decked in sky blues, bright reds, and other hypnotizing tropical colors.

"Nothin'." I sighed. "It's just a lot." I planted a kiss on her forehead then planted her heeled feet on the ground.

"How much was all this?" I had to ask. My Pops would have a heart attack if he knew I'd let a woman foot the bill for something as special as this.

"Does it matter?" Taya hiked a brow, heels clicking as she made her way to the wall of windows at the other end of the living room. "Come look at this view. It's beautiful." I could hear the smile in her voice and for that reason alone, I shook off whatever I was feeling and joined her at the window.

"It *is* nice." I stepped up behind her, pulling her braids over her shoulder to expose the side of her neck, the perfect spot to land a kiss.

"But in the future…" I started, placing a gentle kiss on her warm skin. "Could you give me a heads up? I don't want you thinking you gotta pay for everything. Or *anything*, for that matter."

"If it means that much to you, I will." She turned around and looked up into my eyes. "You got any more preferences before we…"

"Before we what?"

"Before we…*continue*."

"Oh, I got several preferences." I grinned, and she did too, arms up and around my neck as I grabbed her by the waist and slid my tongue between her lips.

I could already tell that a little bit of Taya wasn't gonna be enough. That the way her ass fit perfectly in my hungry palms wasn't gonna be something I could do without for days. This was dangerous, being this close to her. Having her body and giving her mine exclusively. I was equally anxious and scared as hell. You'd swear I was the virgin and she was the one with all the experience.

Taking cues from the way she melted against me, I caressed her behind and sucked her tongue until *it* alone was all that I could taste. She grinded against me, moaning into my mouth, tangling her fingers in my locks as if they were preventing her from floating away. I could feel myself coming to a swell against her belly, and I didn't wanna scare her so I pulled my hips back.

"Don't." She purred against my lips. "I wanna feel you." She peeled her eyes open and stared at me with lust and desperation written all over her face.

"Where's the room?" I asked, taking her hand as she led the way down a short hall where the master suite sat at the end. She pushed the door open to a room about half the size of the space we'd just left, kicking off her heels and trying to reach the zipper at the back of her dress.

"Tay, you gotta slow down." It was almost comical watching her be so hasty about the whole thing.

"But I can't." She whined. *Whined* like a kid. I didn't wanna make her feel worse about it, so I stepped up to help with the dress.

As he sat with his back against the headboard and my back against his chest, I wondered what the hell could be accomplished in this position besides more teasing and no dick. Granted, he'd peeled off everything but my panties and bra, and I could feel his flesh jumping like bass against my back. I wasn't the most experienced in this department, but I was certain this wasn't gonna satisfy my appetite.

Or so I thought.

Just moments before I'd surrendered to being disappointed by the only man who'd brought me to this level of wetness, Chad slid me down until the back of my head was resting against his chest and reached his arms over my breasts until his fingers landed in the seat of my panties.

Teasing me in a way that only he could, he rubbed his thumb over my clit until I purred like a kitten. I was already wet from all the kissing we'd done, nearly embarrassed at how slick I was when he touched me.

"Spread your legs." The depth in his chords rumbled against my neck, forcing me to do as I was told, knees falling to either side, leaving me wide open for him to fondle.

And fondle he did.

Dipping a finger inside me sending sensations of an aching desire to accommodate more than a single digit, he pushed and shoved, gripping my breasts one by one with his free hand, squeezing and sliding until his fingertips pinched my nipples, offering a pain to match the throbbing between my legs. Hungrily, I took his finger into my mouth, sucking it and rocking against his palm, feeding myself to him, readily surrendering my body and likely my soul. So wrapped up in the moment I would've likely said yes to anything he asked for, I tried pulling my knees together to anchor myself but he wouldn't allow it and pushed them apart.

"Fuck!" I shouted, hips raising from the bed as he literally dug into my pussy.

And he didn't say a thing. Just kept on fingering me and biting down on his lip, staring down into my eyes as if my desperation turned him on.

And God, I wanted him so bad.

Feeling the definition of his abs against the back of me and the solidness of his thighs on either side of me was almost enough to drive me insane. I couldn't even regulate my breathing with my legs so far apart and my clit being strummed like a guitar. The intensity of all these feelings rolled up into a ball and dropped to the pit of my stomach rendering me defenseless to whatever was to come.

And then it came.

I came.

All over his hand, leaving a pool of my nectar running down between my legs and soaking my panties. I was crying uncontrollably, both relieved and surprised that under his command, my body could do such a thing. I couldn't even look at him, not until he tugged at my chin and made me, asking if I was okay and assuring me that this was only the tip of the iceberg. I shuttered at the thought that after literally unhinging me with his fingers, there was more.

What the hell have I gotten myself into?

Not giving me a chance to talk myself down off the ledge that I'd so courageously climbed up on, Chad slid from behind me and laid me flat on my back. Words escaped me as he raised up on his haunches and removed his dress shirt one button at a time just to watch me swoon. Smooth, earthy, rich brown skin covered the most amazingly chiseled chest and abdomen I'd been lucky enough to see. In a word, he was beautiful. And he knew that shit too. Staring at me like a meal that he couldn't wait to devour.

And then he did.

Leaning in and bracing his palms on either side of my shoulders, he took my lips into his and then sucked my tongue right out of my mouth. He tasted like he looked, smooth and soothing. I followed his lead feeling somewhere deep inside that it was my only option, tongues tangled in a slippery knot that only the two of us could untangle.

In a seamless motion that would've gone unnoticed had I not been so stimulated by the slightest touch from him, Chad slid a hand under me and unlatched my half-bra, gently pulling it off of me, exposing my nipples to the cool air circulating through the room. I arched my back, relieved that he'd read my mind and took my nipples into his warm mouth one by one, sucking them until they stung them bathing them with his tongue. I moaned, unable to formulate words to express how good it felt to have him touching me and teasing me and exploring me the way he was. Down the symmetry line of my belly was where his tongue traveled next, committing the taste of my skin to memory hopefully with plans to do it again soon. I stared down at the crown of his head with anticipation, running my fingers through his locks, following the waving of his neck as his mouth traveled lower and lower.

And then he arrived there, at the juncture of my thighs, gently parting my knees with the hand that wasn't massaging my breasts. The part of me that had been awakened since the first time I tasted his lips, was separated from his mouth by a thin layer of cloth that would soon be removed. I expected him to be gentle and pull my panties off with his hands the same way he removed my bra. So, imagine my surprise when he turned into a savage and ripped them off with his teeth. I covered my mouth trying to mask how turned on I was that he'd damaged something so delicate with little to no effort. I was not gonna survive this encounter if he did that to my pussy. I needed to call my Mama to make funeral arrangements.

Without words, Chad gave me a look that said, *'This is your last time to get the fuck outta this bed.'* And I countered that look with, *'I ain't never scared.'*

It was a bold-faced lie and I knew it, but lust overcame fear. And as he cast my ruined panties over the side of the bed and dipped his tongue inside me like the serpent that he was, I screamed out loud, giving not one fuck about who might hear me, gripping his locks and holding his face in place.

Taya tasted as good as I thought she would, spread wide open, giving it all to me. I couldn't help looking up at her to see if her face matched the noises leaving her mouth. And it did. The sweetest suffering had contorted her pretty lips into something that I'd been wanting to see for a long, long time.

She dug her nails into my hair and rocked against my lips, the sweetness of her musk filling the room like a flower in bloom. Hungrily, I lapped my tongue over her clit, sucking it into my mouth until it came to a swell. She was feeling it and so was I. Could've stayed there forever if the world outside wasn't still spinning.

"Goddammit!" She bucked and shivered, impending climax coursing through her like blood, forcing her to press harder and harder against my mouth.

Like a fiend, I waited for her to cum again, wanting to taste it and feel it and see it in her eyes. The most selfless act I'd ever exercised was right there in that bed, giving of myself with no expectations.

And then it happened.

I could feel her constricting around my finger, trying to squeeze her thighs closed out of fear that she might lose a part of herself during this intense exchange.

And the truth was, she would.

She would absolutely lose a part of herself that wasn't returnable. But we hadn't even gotten to that part yet. This was only a preview.

"Oh my God, I'm gonna cum!" She professed as if I wasn't totally aware. I'd discovered more about her body in the last twenty minutes than she probably knew about herself.

Like how the small of her back was the spot that would help pull her guard down.

And the bend of her neck was where I should kiss for undivided attention.

And that she didn't mind me sucking her nipples until it hurt as long as I covered them in warmth before I trailed down to her belly, which was the part of her that anchored her eyes to mine.

I didn't expect it to be so easy to figure her out. To map out the most effective ways to make love to her before penetration. But I was glad that it was since pleasing Taya beyond trips and expensive gifts was gonna be something I'd need to be proficient at. The only thing a man can give a woman who can have anything she wants is himself, spiritually and physically.

Having tasted as much of her as I could without being a glutton, I slid up the length of her body to kiss her lips then rolled her over on her belly to rub her back.

"You alright?" My chest melted into her back as I whispered in her ear, planting a kiss on her shoulder, sliding out of my slacks and boxers after pulling out my wallet and laying it on the nightstand, exposing my lower extremities to the warmth that was her skin.

She smiled but didn't speak, a direct indication that she wasn't the least bit interested in anything but having me inside of her. So, I reached over and pulled a condom from my wallet, sheeting myself as I hardened against her behind.

Her eyes widened though she tried to stay calm. I craned my neck to take her lips into mine and kissed her until her breathing slowed. Slipping between her cheeks with my hand there to guide, I slid into the softness of her flower, carefully, with consideration of exactly what this was.

"Taya?" My lips brushed her cheek, the tightness of her walls and tension in her body making it hard for me to go in farther.

"Yeah." She replied just above a whisper, body tensing underneath me.

"We can stop if you're not—"

"No." She cut me off. "Please don't stop." She purred, pain and pleasure evident in her tone.

I didn't know if I should feel turned on or guilty, so of course, I chose the former.

Placing gentle kisses down the back of her neck, I grinded against her slowly until the triangle between her thighs spread open. I rolled my hips upward once then twice, experiencing the shattering of the whole damn world as I moved inside, a tear from her eyes falling onto the sheets.

"Taya?" I slid in and out of her body. The fit of her around me couldn't have been more perfect. "You feel so good, baby," I assured her with easy strokes accompanied by tender kisses.

She turned her neck to look back at me, lips parted, eyes glossed, tears subsiding with every thrust. She felt so good and so damn tight, and from the way she started to raise her ass against me, I was relieved to find that this pleasure wasn't all my own.

"*Ahhh.*" She cried out, throwing it back at me as hard as she could, eyes falling closed as her head collapsed against the pillow. "Fuck me, baby!" She begged, allowing me to take her by the wrists and put her hands up over her head.

I rested my weight on the back of her, thighs and chest slick with sweat as I stroked deeper and deeper until I was dizzy from it all. God, what was happening to me? Her whole being was intoxicating. The scent of her. The taste of her. And now the feeling of being deeper inside of her than anyone had ever been. I was losing my mind, fingers locked into hers as I rose up to look down on the glow of her ass while I was buried between her legs. I was damn near in tears at the sight of my sweat dripping down on her back and the need in her voice as she begged me to fuck her harder and stroke her deeper and show no mercy. Every time she cried my name my damn knees felt weak, and before I knew it, all the blood in my body had rushed to the head of my dick.

"*Baby.*" I moaned. *Moaned* like a bitch. Desperate as hell to release, but so concerned with her finishing first that I couldn't. "Taya, baby, please," I begged. The feeling of her tightening around me was more than I could take.

She curled her fists closed, taking mine with them, then buried her face in the pillow to pacify the screams as another orgasm ripped through her body, leaving her wide open and vulnerable to my selfish desires.

I took advantage because I didn't have a choice. Pumping harder and harder, thighs slipping against her ass. My head shot up to the ceiling as untamable grunts left my throat and every ounce of what had been built up in me spilled over inside of her.

Sixteen

"Taya!"

"Shit, you scared me, Bre. I thought you were sleep."

"Why? 'Cause it's four o'clock in the morning? Where the hell've you been?"

I kicked off my heels as quietly as I could and grabbed a pair of pajamas from the chest of drawers that Bre and I had been sharing during our stay in the mansion.

"Taya?"

"What?"

"I know you heard me. Where the hell were you all night? Your mama was tiptoeing around here like a thick ass cat burglar."

"What? Are you serious?" I whispered, not wanting to wake anybody since me and Chad had barely snuck in.

"No. But if she was, you woulda been caught." Bre rolled her eyes, the light from the bathroom barely illuminating her face as she lay in bed wearing a bonnet as usual.

"Whatever. I'm grown." I smacked my lips, flopping down on the bed after turning off the bathroom light.

"Sounds good." Bre rolled over on her back. "But grown people don't sneak in after riding dick all night."

"Bre!"

"Don't *Bre* me. Even with the lights off, I can see your ass walking funny. Was he big?"

"Seriously?"

"Yes, *seriously*." I could see her eyes bucking from across the room. "You ain't even gotta say it. That smile on your face is all the answer I need. Just tell me one thing, did you do the hula hoop on it?"

"Bre, go to sleep." I slid down into my bed, pulling the covers up to my waist after finding a comfortable position that soothed the throbbing between my legs.

"Fine, I will." She smacked her lips. "I know how it feels to be fucked into exhaustion. But this ain't over."

"Thank you. And good night." I sighed, though sleeping was the last thing I was about to do.

All I could think about was Chad and how much I was willing to risk to run downstairs and sneak into his room.

But I couldn't.

Didn't wanna seem desperate or sex-crazed. Never in a million years had I expected my first time to be so amazing and I couldn't help wondering if every time would be that good.

"Bre?"

"What? I thought you were sleepy."

"I am. But I can't go to sleep."

"Why not? Regret keeping you up?" She yawned and stretched, pulling her phone off the nightstand.

"Fuck you." I giggled. "And it's the opposite of regret, actually."

"Oh, so it *was* good?" She laid her phone back down and turned her head to the side, smiling at me.

"So good." I hoped she couldn't hear the desperation in my voice. But even if she could, oh well.

"Gimme the deets, freak. Did you hula hoop on the dick like I told you?" She turned on her side and propped her head in her palm.

"No."

"What? Man, you weak." She pssh'd me.

"I'm not ready for all that," I smirked. I seriously wasn't.

"Oh, so now you wanna be a kid? I thought you just said you was grown."

"And I am."

"Then woman up and ride that dick before ya man get took."

"Bre, you don't understand. I…it's just. It's a lot."

"Alotta what?"

"Alotta *dick*, fool. I'm not tryna give myself a hysterectomy."

"Whoa! Preacher boy got a mule? I knew it!" The girl was almost clapping, sitting straight up in bed and throwing the covers off her legs.

"Would you calm down, fool? My mama's probably right outside the door." I shook my head.

"My bad." She composed herself, kind of. Still smiling like a Cheshire cat.

"And what made you think he was packing? I mean aside from the fact that you're a pervert."

"Easy. He walks slow." She straightened her bonnet.

"Wait, what?"

"Girl, it's the easiest tell sign. Niggas with big dicks don't never get in a rush. I bet he even drives slow. 'Cause he knows whatever bitch he's on his way to is gon' wait." She tilted her head to the side and snapped. And I almost hollered laughing.

Sadly, she was right. Because from this day forward, I would probably be the bitch sitting on the edge of my bed waiting for Chad *and* his dick.

"Whatever." Of course, I couldn't admit that out loud. Bre would never let me live it down if I admitted to being whipped.

"Mm-hm." She pressed her lips together, pulling her covers in place and laying back down. "Ain't no shame in being *dick-matized*, sis. I just pray the Lord sends some meat my way."

"So, you praying for dick now?" I would say I couldn't believe she'd said that, but that would be a lie.

"I'm not tryna be trifling but the Saints say be specific in your prayer. Ask Chad." She shimmied a shoulder and pulled the covers up to her chest.

"You stupid." I chuckled, climbing out of bed because I wasn't about to get a wink of sleep anyway. "I'mma go downstairs and get a water. You good?"

"Yeah, I'm good." She peeped over her shoulder. "Don't slip and fall on no dick down there." She added before I headed out the door, laughing my ass off.

"Hey, Mama. What you doin' up?" I almost dropped my phone, having just sent a text to Chad to meet me by the pool since neither of us were finding it easy to go to sleep.

"I was thirsty." She pulled the refrigerator open, looking back at me at the kitchen island and rolling her eyes. "I'd ask you the same question if I didn't know the answer."

"What? I was thirsty too." I cleared my throat, trying to be slick and shoot Chad a warning to abort the mission.

"I bet you are." Mama huffed.

"So we swimming or skinny—Um, hey Ms. Tashena." Chad rounded the corner and cleared his throat. I wished like hell I could melt into the floor.

"Sit down," Mama demanded the both of us as she took a seat in one of the comfy barstools on the opposite side of the island. "I don't know if that sounded like a request, but it wasn't. Sit your asses down so we can get this over with."

"Get what over with?" I asked like an idiot. I knew this woman like the back of my hand and she knew me just as well.

"You sure you wanna play with me at damn near five o'clock in the morning, Taya?" She did that thing with her eyes that had signaled an impending ass whooping when I was little.

I hadn't forgotten.

"Mama,"

"Ms. Tashena,"

"Would y'all stop?" She cut us both off. "You're grown. And if you spent the night fucking until the clock struck twelve, that's your business and I don't care."

"Oh my God!" I slid off the stool and stood up, hand over my face to hide the embarrassment. Chad looked like he wanted to run. But he didn't. Just sat there and took it.

"Were you careful?" I was standing with my arms folded across my chest, refusing to answer my mother though she was staring straight at me.

"Fine, I'll ask him. Chad, were you careful with my daughter's vagina?" She slanted her eyes to him. And I didn't expect him to reply because my mama was freaking crazy.

"Yes, ma'am I was. *We* were." He didn't stutter. "I mean, you *are* asking if we used protection, right?"

"What the hell!?" I shrieked. "Look, you don't have to do this. Mama, please."

"What else would I be talking about? You one of them whips and chains typa niggas? You tryna beat my baby?"

"Mama, please stop!" I hurried over beside her. "Chad, you do *not* have to entertain this."

He smiled nervously, running a hand down his chin.

"I hope you ain't this stuck up in the bedroom." Mama kept going. "Tryna act all modest with your skin glowing like a Butter Ball. I'm your mother. You don't think I'd know? Didn't think I'd see that glow from the other side of the kitchen?"

"I don't doubt that you would notice anything, Mama. I just don't feel comfortable talking about it right now." I took a deep breath and blew it out, hoping she'd take the hint and leave it alone.

"And why not?" She wasn't done.

"Because!" I whined. "Chad is not your son and I'm sure he doesn't wanna discuss his...*activities* with you. You barely even know each other."

"I know him well enough to not hide my purse in his presence."

"What does that even mean, Mama?" I slumped my shoulders, eyes rolling from her to Chad while he sat there with the same grin on his face like this conversation didn't bother him in the least bit.

"Calm down, child." She said. "It means I trust him. And even if I didn't, you're both grown. I didn't mean to embarrass you. It's just kind of what I do." She leaned to the side and hooked an arm around my waist, planting a kiss on my cheek before I could lean my head in the opposite direction.

"Is Kenny up? I could use him now to drag you outta here." I looked up at her after she pecked my cheek again and released me from her hold.

"Kenny is currently covered in sleeping babies, scared to move out of fear that one of 'em might wake up." She shook her head.

"Taya!" A little voice came screaming from the other side of the kitchen where Mama and Kenny's room was.

"Hey, Oakley! What you doin' up?" I braced myself as my

almost-three-year-old step-sister came crashing into me, roping her arms around my hips.

"Charlie boo booed and it's stinky." She said with her little nose scrunched, jet-black curls peeping from under a yellow bonnet that matched her yellow pajamas.

"Lord. Is Daddy changing him?" Mama sighed.

"Yes, ma'am." Oakley nodded, looking back at Mama, arms still wrapped around me.

"Let me go in here and give this man a break," Mama said.

"Can I sleep in your room, Taya?" Oakley asked like she'd been doing every night since we got to the mansion.

"Oakley, I don't think Taya's going to bed right now. Come on. You can see her in the morning." Mama reached out a hand, but Oakley didn't budge.

"But I don't wanna sleep in there." Oakley wined. "Charlie, Taj and Mac have Daddy all covered up."

"So, you don't wanna cuddle with me?" Mama propped a hand on her hip, slanting her eyes down at Oakley and pretending to be sad.

"I *do* like to cuddle with you." Oakley turned around and looked her straight in the eyes, still holding on to the leg of my pajama bottoms. "But I didn't see Taya all day. I missed her in my heart." She pointed to her little chest and it was all I could do not to laugh.

"Somebody's gonna be a lawyer one day." Mama shook her head, eyes sliding up to me from Oakley. "Do you mind?" She asked me.

"Of course, I don't. And I missed you too little woman." I rubbed a hand over Oakley's bonnet.

"I guess it's settled then," Mama said. "Come get your blanket, Maxine Shaw." She teased.

"And Chad," Mama stopped in her tracks as Oakley tor away from me to go retrieve her favorite blanket.

"Yes, ma'am." Chad gave her his undivided attention.

"Be careful not to overindulge." This woman was really a piece of work. "You look tired as hell and I know why. She gets it from her mama." She shimmied. *Shimmied* as she walked away, laughing like a hyena while I stood there, knowing I couldn't do anything but let her be.

"I hope you don't mind the extra company."

Chad and I had gone out to sit by the pool with Oakley Rose tagging along before she fell asleep in one of the lounge chairs.

"It's cool. I'm used to having my niece around. So…"

"That's right. You're a super uncle." I relaxed in the comfy patio sofa after tucking Oakley's blanket around her.

"I wouldn't say all that." Chad slid closer to me, pulling my feet up on his lap.

"I would. I'd say you're super everything, actually." I caught his eyes in the tiny space between us. "And that's why I love you."

I swear on every star in the sky that I did not intend to say that out loud. It sort of slipped out while he was massaging my feet. All kinds of shit was bound to slip out when Chad's hands were on me.

"I'm sorry." I pulled my feet away when he chose silence over a response.

"What? It's cool." He stared at me. Stared *through* me, to be exact. And I could feel the world stopping on its axis, waiting for me to breathe.

And in the middle of all that, my phone pinged. Then one ping was followed by ten until it wouldn't stop pinging at all.

"What's going on?" Chad let go of my feet as I picked my phone up off the side table.

"I...this is. Oh my God!" I burst into tears, pulling my feet from his lap and hopping up off the sofa.

"I can't believe this! This mother fucker!" I screamed, taking off toward the house with my chest on fire.

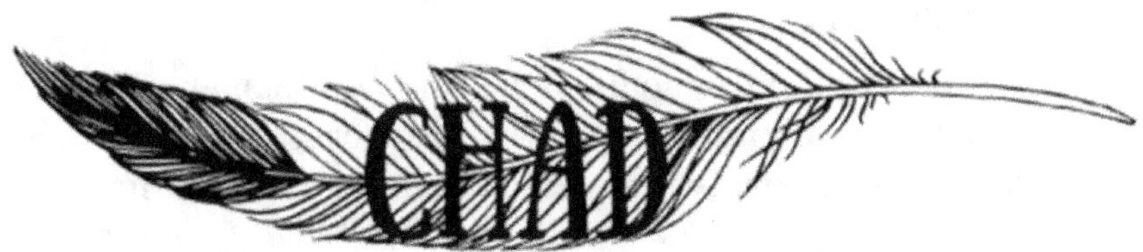

"Taya, no!" I heard Tashena's voice as I rushed into the house after picking Oakley up and carrying her inside. I had no idea what Taya had seen on that phone, but soon after, my phone started ringing like crazy. I didn't have time to answer it trying to find Taya to see what was up. But I soon found out when I made it inside and stopped at the bottom of the stairs.

"You fuckin' piece of shit! I trusted you!" She was at the top of the staircase all in Jock's face. He looked like he'd been woken up from a deep sleep and didn't know what she was talking about. I still didn't know what was going on and dude looked like he didn't know either.

"Taya, I swear, I didn't post that shit!" Jock yelled, jumping back when Taya tried to swing on him.

"Taya, stop." At this point, Tashena had run past me while I stood there not knowing what to do with a sleeping toddler in my arms. Plus wasn't far behind her, ascending the steps in lightning speed, pulling Taya and Tashena back away from Jock. Oakley was still sleeping like a log in my arms, so I went over to the living room and laid her down on the sectional.

"Why would you do this, Jock?" Taya's voice was shaky. "I thought we were better than that." She bawled.

"Taya, I swear—"

"Don't lie to me!" She tried pulling away from Plus's hold. "Who else would have those pics? You're the only one I sent them to!"

She was breathing so hard it scared me. Looked like she was about to hyperventilate.

"Just go downstairs, alright." Plus stepped between Jock, Taya, and Tashena.

"You better do somethin' with him." Tashena pointed in Jock's face before walking Taya down the steps. "Fuckin' idiot." She pulled Taya in against the side of her, roping an arm around her waist.

"Chad, do you mind sitting with Oakley while I calm her down?" Tashena asked in a hurry.

And of course, I said yes, still in the dark about the details of all the drama going on.

"Everything alright?" Plus finally came downstairs after talking with Jock for about twenty minutes. Apparently, according to a stream of texts from my sisters, someone had uploaded nudes of Taya on the internet, and Taya said Jock was the only one who'd had them.

"I'on't know, man." Kenny picked up Oakley and laid her over his shoulder before taking a seat next to me. "Shit's crazy. He's sayin' he didn't do it. And he's a lotta things, but he ain't never lied to me."

"So, what're y'all gonna do have him arrested? She said he's the only one with the pics, right?" I was one hundred degrees hot about this shit. And the only thing stopping me from running up the stairs and wiping the floor with that nigga was the fact that Plus was standing behind his innocence and remaining calm while doing so.

"I wish it was that easy, bruh." He said. "It'd be a dream come true if I could just go up there and kick dude's ass. But I really don't think he did it. Him and Taya squashed their li'l beef before the tour wrapped. They both told me."

"Damn." That was the only response I could muster. Taya was in the room probably crying her damn eyes out and this cat was probably upstairs feeling nothing at all.

"Yeah." Plus returned. "I could definitely live without all this shit."

He sighed, patting his daughter's back as I got up off the couch. "She probably won't want to, but could you tell Taya to holler at me?"

"Bet." He nodded, slapping into a handshake as I headed off to the room I was sharing with Sabre.

"Man, this shit is crazy." Sabre was sitting up in bed when I walked in. "You talked to Taya yet?"

"Nah." I rubbed my head, kicking my slides off at the foot of the bed. "I'm sure she ain't in the mood for talking right now. Ya boy's wild, man."

"That he is." Sabre looked up from his cell before putting it down on the nightstand. "But I'on't think he did this though."

"Man, not you too." I flopped down on the queen-sized bed that was so comfortable it had me tryna figure out how to stuff it in my luggage and fly it back home. "Plus said the same thing. And I don't know if y'all have been paying attention, but it doesn't seem far-fetched for this nigga to pull off something like this."

"Makes sense that you'd think that since you've only witnessed him beefing with Taya. But Jock's pretty solid. Nigga just needs to put down the bottle for the rest of his life."

"Whatever." I flipped the covers back and slid my legs under them, back propped against the tufted linen headboard as I flipped out my phone to see if I'd missed any messages from Taya.

None.

"It's about to be awkward as hell around here for the next coupla days." Sabre sighed. "This was supposed to be a relaxing trip to celebrate our accomplishments, now we're all gonna be eating in silence watching everybody shoot side-eyes at Jock. Stupid."

"You really don't believe he did it, huh?"

"Hell no," Sabre said, fluffing his pillow.

"This is the same cat who disrespected you in Bottoms. Since when do we give passes for disrespect, Sabe? You changing out here?"

"This is coming from the mouth of the son of a minister? You trippin' bro." He fell back against his pillow and slanted his eyes at me.

"Man, I'm just sayin'. He handled you."

"He was drunk. The man's allergic to alcohol and needs to seek help. I can't hold that against him. Not when I got my own shit to deal with."

"Man. You really do vouch for this cat."

"I do," Sabre replied. "And do the same for you if you were accused of some shit like this."

"That's good to know." I checked my phone one more time. Still nothing. "Luckily for you, I canceled the potential of seeing any more nudes the minute I agreed to come on this trip."

"Yeah?" Sabre's voice hiked. "You throwin' in your playa's card, bruh?"

"That's what it feels like." I took a deep breath, dropping my phone on the nightstand and easing down into the bed. "That's sure as hell what it feels like."

Seventeen

I wanted to disappear. To curl up in a ball and fade away because it felt like the whole world could see me, and not in a good way. Chad and Sabre had tried a few times to come in and check on me but I wasn't fit to face them or anybody else. Well, except for Bre since Mama'd put her on security duty.

And speaking of my mama, she'd taken my phone so I could rest, or sulk, or whatever she thought I should do instead of reading every single blog on the internet in the wake of my naked body being exposed. I barely heard her suggestions under the fog of my thoughts, and she should've known that as her daughter, I wasn't about to sleep on this shit. As soon as she left my room, I picked up Bre's phone while she used the bathroom and navigated my way to the original post that I took a screenshot of and texted to her before it was deleted.

I didn't initially pay attention to the caption under the pic. But now that I'd calmed down, something about it was strange.

PLP.

Three letters that wouldn't mean shit to anybody who saw them. Except for one person. The one who'd written them under my picture in our high school yearbook and at the end of every text thread we ever exchanged.

"Why the hell would she do this?" I thought to myself. And more importantly, why would she leave such an incriminating clue? Hadn't she brought enough drama to my life already? Did the bitch have a walking death wish?

"Hey, where you goin'?" Bre came out of the bathroom just as I was climbing out of bed.

"To kill Kanika. You comin?" I stood up and tightened the band that was holding my ponytail in place.

"Yep. Lemme get my shoes." Bre hurried around to the side of her bed, sliding into a pair of pink Plus flip flops. "Why we killin' this bitch again?" She pulled a bonnet from a drawer in her nightstand and secured it over her waist-length loose waves.

"I'll tell you later. Wassup with the bonnet?" I had to ask. Even in the heat of the moment, I needed to pick Bre's crazy brain.

"In case there's blood." She replied like it was a normal answer and I smirked.

"What? These bundles cost too much to be gettin' skank blood on em." She pulled the bonnet down a little more and headed toward the door.

"Kanika, open up." With Bre on the lookout for my mama, we made it up the steps to Kanika's room without being caught.

"We got lettuce!" Bre randomly yelled and I looked at her like she was crazy. "What? You know the bitch don't eat nothin' but lettuce. I'm tryna help."

"Well, you're not." I squinted.

"Whatever." She rolled her eyes.

Then "Yes?" the door opened and there she was, in all her trifling glory. Showing no remorse for what had gone down, further validating my assumption that her ass was guilty.

"You comin' in or…"

"No." I quickly responded. "Bre, lemme see your phone." I extended a hand without breaking eye contact with Kanika.

"Dog, I just got this one. You tryna crack it over her head? 'Cause I can go get Sabre's or somethin'."

"Bre, the phone. *Please!*" I commanded, the taste of salt curling in my mouth.

"Fine." She hesitantly handed me her cell. "If you break it, Lettuce gotta pay for it."

"Could somebody please tell me why y'all are at my door?" Kanika folded her arms and asked.

"To kill you apparently. I'm not sure why." Bre replied.

"I'm here because of *this*." I pulled up the pic and held the phone in front of Kanika's face.

"What, your tits?" She smirked. "I've seen 'em already. The whole damn world has seen 'em."

"Tay, not that it matters, but can you please fill me in on exactly what the fuck is goin' on here?" Bre stepped up beside me and whispered.

"*PLP*." I stared at Kanika and said. "*Perfect Little Princess*. Only one person in the world would use that caption. And she's standing right in front of me, pretending to be innocent when she knows for a fact she is everything but that."

"Shit." Bre's mouth fell open.

"You're crazy and I don't have time for this shit." Kanika turned around and was about to slam the door in my face before I stepped in front of it, walking right into her room, grabbing a handful of her hair and yanking her out into the hallway.

"Let me go!" Kanika kicked and screamed while I pulled her

hair so hard her neck snapped back.

"Oh shit, you really tryna kill the bitch!" Bre flew into action after I banged Kanika's head against the wall not once but twice.

"Taya, stop!" Bre yelled. "It's not worth it." She pulled my arms.

I blacked out in a fit of rage for God knows how long. And the next thing I saw was Jock running over to help Bre pull me off Kanika after I'd thrown her to the ground, straddled her waist and beat her face until my knuckles were sore. I broke down in Bre's arms, barely able to catch my breath. Voices around me were all muffled and the rest was a blur.

"Well, at least she's not filing charges." Things had calmed down as much as they were going to and Mama wasn't letting me out of her sight until we boarded the plane back to Houston.

"Filing charges for what? She brought that shit on herself." I fumed, sitting on the edge of her bed watching Oakley Rose play peek-a-boo with the triplets.

"First of all, watch your mouth." Mama glared at me. "And second, did you see that girl's head?" Her eyes widened and I almost busted out laughing.

"No, I haven't. You got me locked in here, remember?" I sighed, closing my eyes and falling back on the bed, immediately feeling a baby crawling on my face.

"Well, she looks like Martin in that episode when Tommy Hitman 'Hearns' Martin got ahold of him."

"Are you serious?"

"Dead ass."

"Well, she deserved it." I sat up to peel Mac off of my head, grabbing a burp rag from the side table to wipe her drool off my cheek and her mouth.

"I agree." Mama reached to the foot of the bed to pull Taj from the edge in one seamless motion. "Be that as it may, we don't need you racking up assault charges. It's just not a good look."

"What's not a good look is having my tatas splattered all over the internet." I got heated all over again just thinking about it.

"And I agree with that too. And we're already taking steps to file charges. However, if you file on her, you can guarantee she's gonna file on you."

"And?" I smirked, planting a kiss on Mac's chubby cheek before putting her back down and watching her crawl over to her giggling siblings.

"*And,* nothing if you don't mind being labeled *The Thugged Out Princess of R&B*."

"I'll gladly take that label. Especially since the alternative is being labeled a weak b-word who got crossed by a fake friend and did nothing about it."

I got where my mama was coming from, but I wasn't sorry for what I'd done. And just like the world had seen my tits, they were gonna see the consequences of playing with me.

"I guess." She took a deep breath and blew out. "Looks like a little bit of me rubbed off on you after all." She picked up Charlie when a strange smell invaded the room. "I love you, lil girl." She looked up at me and said.

"I love you too." I returned with a wink. "And can I please leave while you change your son? He smells like a grown man."

"Yeah. *Cha Cha!*" She yelled toward the door, and Cha Cha showed up in lightning speed. "Can you please follow Tupac around for me? We don't need her racking up no more charges."

Cha Cha nodded yes, of course, following me out by the pool where the rest of The Crew, minus Kimi, was sitting probably discussing how bad I'd messed up Kanika's face.

"Y'all out here talkin' about me?" I stepped out onto the patio, easing down on the foot of the lounge chair Bre was sitting in.

"Chill, Mayweather, we don't want no smoke." Sabre teased, putting his hands up and blocking his face.

"Shut up!" I chunked a small pillow at him, laughing before I turned my focus to Jock who hadn't said a peep.

"Jock, I'm sorry." There was no need in waiting to say it. "I shoulda heard you out and I was wrong."

"It's all good." He shrugged.

"You're still trifling for flying her out here though," I added with a smirk.

"Trifling as hell," Bre added.

"That was a trash move, bro." Even Sabre chimed in, which was a shock since he had his boy's back through every single thing.

"So, y'all ganging up on me now?" Jock pressed his hands to his chest, a slither of a smile tracing his pink lips.

"Yes!" Bre piped. "Flew that girl all the way out here to get her face rearranged. That's ten different *kinds* of trifling."

Jock chuckled. "Aight, I was wrong." He confessed.

"Was somebody recording that?" I squinted.

"Man, get off the gas." Jock chuckled again.

And as the mood went from cold to warm around us, I suddenly noticed that someone was missing.

"Where's Chad?" I asked, looking toward the patio door, certain that he'd walk out at the mention of his name.

"Probably in his room making sure he didn't do something that would make you wanna *Kanika* his face." Bre joked.

Jock laughed but Sabre didn't.

"Sabe, was he in the room?" I sensed something telling in his demeanor. "Sabe?" I repeated when he didn't look up, all of a sudden super interested in something on his phone.

"Nah." He replied without looking at me.

"Then, where is he?" I asked, on my way to frustration.

"He left." Sabre sighed, dropping his phone in his lap. "He went home. I thought he told you. He said he told—"

"He didn't tell me." I slid forward at the end of the chair. "Why? Why would he leave? And *now* of all times. Did I do something wrong? I mean aside from two-piecing a bitch who had it coming."

"Nah. I don't... I'on't know, actually. He's not use to all this, I guess." Sabre shrugged.

"And I *am*?" I said. "See, this is why I shoulda left this shit alone in the first place. You act human around a nigga one time and they run back home to their mama."

"Actually, him and his moms are going through a little rift. But—"

"Sabre, do you always have to be so damned literal?" I cut him off.

It didn't matter what Chad had going on at home. What mattered was that I was going through perhaps the worst time of my life, and he couldn't hang around for a few more days to listen and help me through it.

"My bad." Sabre raised both hands.

"No, *my* bad." I got up off the chair to head inside. "That's what I get for opening up again. Lesson number two for the books."

Eighteen

"You did what?"

I don't know why I went to my Pops. But I didn't wanna get chewed out by my sisters and sure as hell didn't want Ma pulling me into the prayer closet.

"It was only a day early, Pops. I had to leave." I tried explaining as I followed him down the corridor to his study. I hadn't even gone home to unpack my luggage. I drove straight to his house from the airport.

"So, where does she think you are?" Pops took a seat in the tall backed, black leather chair that still smelled brand new like the rest of his office furnishings.

"I don't know." I eased into a smaller chair that matched his on the opposite side of the desk.

"Well, has she reached out to you? I'm sure she's worried sick. You just up and left like a thief in the night. I swear, you kids are gonna have people thinking you were raised by the Devil

189

himself."

"I left a note."

"*A note*? Son, you can't be serious. From what your mother tells me you're head over heels for this girl and you couldn't do better than a slip of paper? You didn't get this from me." He shook his head.

"No. No sir." I corrected myself, leaning forward and resting my elbows on my knees. "And did you just say you talked to Mama or am I hearing things?"

"You heard me right." He blew out a breath, easing back in his seat with both fists resting on top of his pecan wood desk. "I've been finding it harder to keep up this grudge every time Boogie comes over telling me how much fun she had at Granny Ma's."

"Well, that's a good sign." I tipped my head up.

"Is it?" He shook his head. "I swear, I never thought I'd see myself in this position. God warned me about *The Valley*, but I sure do wish he would've been more specific. Anyway, this ain't about me. I definitely know where you got your slickness from."

"And where's that?" I huffed out a chuckle, knowing exactly where this was going.

"Your Uncle Jimmy." He looked off to the side as if he were imagining his younger brother standing there, though he'd been long gone before me or my sisters were born.

"Yeah, Jimmy could slick a can of oil." He remembered. "I never saw anybody lie their way out of a butt whooping like he did. That is until I was tasked with raising *you*." He returned his eyes to his one and only son who was sitting in the midst of a situation that he couldn't grasp if he had a thousand hands.

"So, did you come here to ask me what you should do, or have you decided and need me to agree with you?" He folded his big hands together.

"Actually, Pops, I just need some advice," I replied.

"And don't you typically go to your mother for that?" He returned with a tone that teetered on the lines of jealousy.

"Yeah, but this is different," I said. "And I'm hoping you can guide me 'cause at this point, even God's probably frustrated with the situation."

"Oh, I doubt that." He huffed. "But I'm honored that you'd tug at these old ears. So, what's the problem?"

Man, I hadn't even thought of how to word it. It wasn't just one thing at this point. It was a world of things that had my head spinning like crazy.

"Okay, so, I love Taya." I started the best way I knew how. "At least I *think* I do. And that's the problem."

"Okay." He rubbed his fingers together and looked up at the ceiling before returning his eyes to me. "I'm gonna try to stay near the cross when I say this, son, but that doesn't sound like a problem. That sounds like fear."

"But it's not," I responded quickly. "I'm not scared, I'm just not sure."

"I see." He pushed his glasses up off the brim of his nose. "And you expect me to help you with that, how?"

"I don't know."

"Well, you better figure it out, or you're gonna have two problems with no solution."

"Ok, I *know* I love her," I confessed to myself, my father, and God. "And if I can be completely honest, I'm afraid I won't be able to live up to it. Love's a weighty word, Pops."

"And an even weightier action." He nodded. "But it's only as weighty as you make it. And right now, you're putting way too much pressure on yourself."

"I can't help it. I've been doing the wrong thing so long that this feels foreign."

"As it should." My father chuckled. "Change is always awkward. Even painful in some instances. But it's necessary. Getting what you want has been easy all your life, but now it's about getting what you *need*."

I'd never considered that, even though whenever I was around

Taya, it felt like exactly that.

"So, what do I do now that I've sat in here and pulled a whole confessional?"

Pops grinned at me then said "You have to ask yourself why you wanted to be sure. Why you came to me for validation instead of going to your mother. Why do you want this to be love? Does she smell a certain way? Does she walk a certain way? Is there a certain cadence in her voice when she says your name?"

"Yes. Yes, to all of that. But what does that mean? Is that substantial? Does it wear off? Will one of us wake up one day and realize that we ran out of that stuff? I want this so bad, Pops. I want *her* so bad. But I don't wanna make a fool out of myself. I can't wind up like you and…" I stopped when I realized I'd gone too far. That I'd gotten too personal and borderline disrespectful.

"I'm sorry. I didn't mean to—"

"It's okay." He pushed back from his desk. "And now it makes sense why you'd come to me for advice and not your mother. Still doesn't explain why you couldn't pick up the phone and call instead of flying all the way home. But I digress."

He stood from his chair, a tall man who'd been the epitome of God's favor for as long as I could remember. Nobody carried the word with as much passion as he did. Nobody modeled the greatness of the Holy Spirit we all sought better than he did. I was proud to be his son though I sinned and fell short on a daily basis.

"Some things don't translate over the phone." I gave my reason as truthfully and as simply as I could.

"You're smart, Chadwick." He said, stepping up beside me and resting his hand on my shoulder. "Much smarter than I was at your age, that's for sure."

"How so? You were building a following at my age." I looked up at the man who'd passed down to me a set of messy eyebrows that women couldn't seem to get enough of.

"Yeah, I was." He grinned. He had to be proud of himself. "But I wasn't that good at asking the important questions. Didn't quite have the knack for seeing both sides of things. I only saw what I wanted and ignored the obvious if it didn't line up with my plan."

"What do you mean?" I sat straight up in my chair as he took a seat in the chair next to me and looked straight into my eyes.

"This might be hard to hear, son. And I didn't think there'd ever come a day when I'd share this with anybody but God. But I knew I wasn't the man your mother needed. Turns out, no man could've been." He found humor in the situation and I was surprised and impressed.

You could've bought me with a dime and sold me back for a penny, the way those words slipped from his mouth like they'd been sitting there forever.

And they probably had.

Being a leader in the Christian community put burdens on a man's shoulders that were his alone to bear.

"Pops, I—"

"It's alright." He patted my thigh. "It's heavy, I know. But I'm better now. I'm not the same man that I used to be. And though it broke my heart when our marriage dissolved, I can't say I didn't see it coming. Your mother's a special woman for putting up with me, son. For putting her true feelings aside to be with me. To build a family and a congregation with me. And I don't think she'd have it any other way because look at the blessings God gave us in you and your sisters."

"Well, you can thank Him for *me*." I joked. "I don't know about those daughters."

"They're a blessing in their own way." He chuckled. "But my point is, I can't tell you what it is that you're feeling. That's between you, God and this young lady. I pray it's love. It surely looks and sounds like love. And if it is, neither one of you will be able to hide from it too much longer."

"What if it's not?" I didn't expect him to have an answer that would make me feel good about not having Taya in my life, because there wasn't one.

"If it's not," He looked up at a family picture on the

bookshelf. "At least you'll have the memories." He looked back at me, clapping my thigh one more time before he got up out of his seat.

"And if you're lucky, you'll find a God-fearing assistant who knows her way around a pot of collard greens."

"Wait, you talkin' about Sister Bimage?" I squinted. Jada was gonna pass smooth out when I told her about this.

"As a matter of fact, I am." Pops put a little pep in his step heading toward the office door. "Speaking of which, you can let yourself out. I gotta go up and get ready for a uh…friendly dinner. Have a good night, son. I love you."

"Yeah. You too. Love you, Pops."

I got up, shaking my head and shooting a text to Jada, ratting out our Pops for eating Sister Bimage's greens.

Nineteen

Common sense said don't go to her place after I'd made a foolish decision to fly home when she needed me the most.

Common sense told me to chill because according to Sabre, they'd just gotten home, and flights can be exhausting and any response she had to my presence would probably be the result of sleep deprivation and not love.

Common sense told me to leave it alone. To wait until the next day when things were clearer, and I could start the journey of moving on.

But common sense hadn't gotten me anywhere when instincts led me straight to her door.

I'd been standing there for all of one minute when I finally decided to pull my hands out of my pockets. She wasn't answering my calls. Wasn't replying to my texts. For all I knew she could've been in the apartment dead.

Nah, not with Bre there. Not even the dead could sleep through all that yapping.

Having suffered enough, I knocked on the door, and Bre pulled it open almost instantly like she'd been anticipating my visit.

"Were you standing there the whole time?" I asked, standing in front of her, praying that the curve in her lips didn't signal an impending slap upside my head.

"No." She smacked her lips, looking down at a cell in her hand. "The doorbell cam kept chiming, so I checked to see if it was you or that stupid bitch, Kanika. Luckily, it was you." She rolled her eyes.

"Oh." I didn't know how to respond to that so, I didn't. "Is she here?" I looked over Bre's shoulder toward the living room after noticing a pair of tennis shoes on the floor beside the door that were way too big to belong to either of the ladies.

"It depends." She blinked a set of lashes that could double as windshield wipers. "What you got in that bag?"

"Ice cream," I said, remembering that I even had a bag in my hand. "Butter Pecan for you and Pistachio Almond for Taya."

"In that case, she's in her room. Lemme get you a spoon." She spun around on a pair of polka dot pink and purple socks that clashed with her striped pink and white pajamas but still looked surprisingly fly. I hadn't initially seen it upon meeting them for the first time, but Bre and Taya's personalities complimented each other. They were the perfect blend of calm meets storm.

"Before you go in," Bre came out of the kitchen, extending two spoons in my direction. "She thought you might pop up and made me promise not to let you in. But I like you. Any dude that's been friends with Sabre this long without choking him out has to be good people."

I chuckled, taking the spoons and handing her a pint of Butter Pecan ice cream.

"Here's your one chance Fancy, don't let me down." She said, prancing toward Taya's room.

"I won't, *Reba*." I returned, following behind her, probably melting the ice cream with how nervous I was.

"Tay, you got company!" She knocked on the door then pushed it open. "Ain't no knives in here, huh?" She joked.

Taya looked up from her cell, and the look in her eyes messed me up.

"I told you not to—"

"I know. But he brought ice cream." Bre held out her treat. "One for me and one for you. At least hear him out for that. You know it ain't shit in that refrigerator."

"There would be if you'd make a grocery order." Taya still hadn't looked directly at me. And it was taking all the strength I had not to turn around and walk away.

"Come in." She said, after licking her tongue out at Bre.

"Thank you." I looked back at Bre as I stepped into the room.

"Don't fuck this up." Bre dipped her chin at me, then glanced over at her friend and blew her a kiss.

"You need something?" I'd expected her to be cold but not this damn cold. I shoulda stayed my ass at home and just let the whole thing go.

"Actually, I do." I snapped. I hadn't come this far to leave.

"Go ahead."

"Can I sit?"

"I don't know. Do you want to?" She shrugged her shoulders, sitting with her back against the headboard.

"I deserve that." I pulled the door closed behind me. "And I'm sorry. I shouldna left like that. I shouldna left at all."

"Yeah, but you *did*." She sighed. "And now you show up at my door with ice cream, of all things, seeking forgiveness. Does that usually work?"

"On who?"

"On women."

"I don't know." I quickly replied. "Never tried it."

"Oh, that's right. 'Cause you got dick." Her eyes went wide as she flipped the covers off her legs and climbed out of bed.

"I don't know what you came for and you probably don't either." She walked past me, looking me up and down before heading into an en suite bathroom. "And the ice cream is a nice gesture, but you can leave it in the freezer. I don't have much of an appetite." She yelled from the bathroom where she was apparently taking a leak.

Was she that comfortable around me?

"What makes you think I don't know why I came here?" I stood at the foot of her bed, canvasing all the décor on her walls, mostly red with splashes of black and yellow.

"Because you don't." She stood in front of the bathroom mirror, looking up at my reflection standing behind her as she washed her hands. "And I get it. Especially since my life's a mess right now with my tits splattered all over social media. Who'd wanna deal with that, right?" She dried her hands on a crimson bath towel, the slight shiver in her voice making it obvious that she was trying not to cry.

"Not that it matters to me, because it doesn't," I said as she walked out of the bathroom and flopped down on her bed. "I don't care about that. And the world won't either in a few weeks. It's just another thing. Another shitty person doing shitty things when they don't get what they want. Or in this case, *who* they want."

She pulled a bottle of lotion that came in the kit I'd sent her from Angela's natural product line and rubbed it over her hands and wrists, unaware of how even *that* had me hypnotized.

"If only it were that easy." She looked over at me and said.

"It is that easy. It can be that easy of you'll let me—"

"Let you what, Chad?" She cut me off, hands planted on her thighs, chocolate skin glowing. "You've already shown me that when shit gets thick your first instinct is to run and hide. And should I expect a note next time too? A damn note instead of coming to me and telling me you're leaving? Not only was I humiliated, I found out that my own damn friend was the one who posted the pics. And you know what I'm gonna get from that? A brand new mugshot for leaving a big ass knot upside her head. And I had to go through that without you. Without the person I'd literally given myself to because I thought you were worth it. Thought you were worth my time. Turns out you're just a fucking coward." She rolled her eyes, sliding back into bed and pulling the covers up to her waist. "You can leave now. And take that melted ass ice cream with you."

"Taya…"

"Go! Please. I'm tired."

"I can't." I put the ice cream down on a desk on the other side of her room. "And I'm sorry about the shit with Kanika, but I didn't come all the way over here just to walk out feeling the same emptiness I felt before I saw you."

"Seriously? I'm not in the moo—"

"And I don't mean before tonight." I kept going because I had to. Something was fueling me to do so. Could've been the Holy Spirit. Could've been the full moon. Hell, for all I know, it could've been love.

Whatever it was, I had found it in her eyes and there was no way I was leaving her room, her home, her thoughts before I said what I'd come to say.

"That night at Bottoms," I started from the beginning which was typically the best part of any love story. "The outfit is fuzzy 'cause I was mostly staring in your face."

I lied.

That shit was black and tight and had been the object of my fantasies for damn near the past year.

"But you were wearing red lipstick, which happens to be my favorite color."

She rested her head on her knuckle and stared at me, not saying a word.

So, I went on.

"I mean no disrespect when I say this, but I never questioned whether or not I could get your number that night." I fought the urge to grin because this was possibly the most serious conversation I'd ever had. "But I was still nervous, cause I was me and you were you and the math just didn't add up. If anything, it would've turned out to be a chance encounter, you'd get bored or I'd get distracted and that would be the end of Chad and Taya. But it didn't turn out that way."

I paused to clear my throat. I still wasn't comfortable spilling my emotions in front of people. Yet here I was, standing at the foot of a woman's bed getting choked up while trying to convince her that we were meant to be together.

"I came here to tell you I love you." I continued with her eyes glued to me and glistening. "I'm sorry I didn't say it then, the first time I saw you. But in my defense, I probably would've looked crazy."

"Kinda how you look now?" She smiled, barely. But that was enough.

"Are you sure?" She sat straight up in bed.

"Yes, I'm sure." A ball of emotion churned in my throat and before I knew it, a tear was sliding down my cheek. "You think I'd be standing here crying like an idiot over somebody I don't love?" I'd forgotten I had hands, or feet for that matter, as she got up and walked over to me, sliding a thumb across my cheek to erase my tears.

"Say it." I leaned in and whispered against her lips. "Say it so I know I'm not in this by myself."

"You're not." Her voice quivered. A nigga was getting another chance. "I love you." She said as I stared down into her eyes. Eyes that I thought would never be mine to look into again.

"But if you ever walk out on me again—"

"I won't." I sliced right through her words. "I swear."

He didn't smile, instead choosing to cup his hands on either side of my face, pulling me into a kiss that melted down into the middle of me, sending my heart racing into a rhythm of intangible ecstasy.

I didn't breathe for the duration of this passionate exchange, surrendering to his hands as he pushed my shorts down around my hips. I slipped out of them so fast it was a God damn shame. I was as hungry for his body as he was for mine. His touch warmed me from the inside out, fingertips dragging up my sides as he rolled my tank top up and off. My nipples came to attention like two caged birds when he reached around to unlatch my bra, freeing my breasts and staring down at them. He took me in, eyes canvasing my body from the tips of my toes to the crown of my head. My chest caved and expanded as I wept, so happy to be in his presence, naked and his for the taking.

Chad stepped back an inch to disrobe and my wet eyes ballooned at the sight of his mahogany flesh. He was beautiful in a way that could and should be photographed, lines of definition accenting the V below his waist and the contours of his arm and thigh muscles. My mouth watered, salty tears falling from my eyes to the bed of my lips. If this wasn't love, standing here naked and crying because I couldn't wait another minute to have him inside me again, I honestly didn't know what was.

Closing the space between us, he roped his arms around my waist and squeezed me so tight that I almost couldn't breathe. He smashed his lips against mine, licking them and sucking them until an involuntary moan left my mouth and swam over his tongue. He tasted divine, strong and sure and all fucking mine. He slid a hand up the middle of me, starting at the peak of my sex and landing with a clap around my neck. Full control of my body was relinquished as he choked me, firm but gently, sucking my tongue like it belonged to him.

And it did.

I did.

There was nothing in the world that had ever felt better, warmer, or more perfect than the firmness of Chadwick Fold Jr's body pressed against mine. A blink from his lashes nearly set me on fire when he trailed a kiss from my lips, down my chin, and down both sides of my neck. My knees went weak and the butterflies in my belly flew free. I was a fraction of the angry woman that he'd walked in on.

Hoisting me up of the floor and wrapping my legs around his waist, he blindly carried me to the bed and laid me down on my back, all while completely devouring my mouth, speaking to me in a way that didn't require words. I hadn't stopped crying since I started, and he didn't feel the need to ask why. And that was a good thing because the answer wouldn't've made sense anyway.

Because how could I explain that I was crying because he felt so good?

How could it possibly make sense that I was crying because I was overjoyed?

How would he comprehend that my tears were fluid gratitude?

Who on earth could grasp the concept of a woman crying because she knew exactly what it felt like to fall in love?

As my thoughts swam to places that were only making more tears fall, Chad pushed my knees apart and licked his lips as the pinkness of my sex lay unpantied and exposed. I pulled my bottom lip between my teeth, heat curling in my belly, nipples as solid as rocks with his stare burning my skin. He leaned forward, resting his weight on his palms, chest barely touching my breasts as he kissed my lips, along my collar bone, sucked both nipples, then trailed all the way down between my legs.

And *"Oh!"* I moaned as he sucked my clit hard before soothing it slowly, dragging a struggled breath from my lungs, pushing my legs open before the initial reaction of being overly stimulated forced them closed around his head. I raised my hips from the bed, rocking and rolling and gliding against his face, losing my breath when his tongue darted inside me, licking me deeper into submission.

There were no waterworks this time, but it was embarrassing how fast I came on his face. He rose from between my thighs with the glow of my nectar on his beautiful lips and I couldn't wait to taste it. Couldn't wait to suck myself off his tongue. Sliding up the length of my body, he smiled and planted a gentle kiss on my lips as I reached over into a drawer on my nightstand to retrieve a condom, unashamed of the fact that even though I was pissed at him for leaving without saying goodbye, something deep inside me hoped he'd come over to make things right.

"Why you lookin' at me like that?" That sexy grin hadn't left his face and he had no idea what it did to me.

"I can't look at you?" My lips curled to the side, chills traveling from the back of my neck to the tips of my toes when his chuckle vibrated against me.

"You can do whatever you wanna do to me." He said before parting my lips with his tongue then pulling away to stare down at me.

Typically, I would've taken those words with a grain of salt. Wouldn't have done more than smile with appreciation. But lying there next to Chad, having full access to all that he was, a loud voice screamed in both of my ears, *"Climb on top and hula hoop that dick!"*

So, I did.

Following the verbal commands of my crazy ass friend, I slid from under Chad's arm and positioned myself on top of him.

"What you doin'?" He looked and sounded confused.

"What does it look like I'm doin'?" I tried to act confident but on the inside, I was scared as hell.

"Taya—"

"This is what I want." I cut him off. "Gimme." I reached a hand out for the condom that I'd handed him and he hesitantly ripped it open and handed it to me. The next round of nervous energy shot through me when I took him into my hand and slid the condom down over him.

He was big.

And I knew that already, obviously, but actually having him in my grip made it that much more intimidating. Could I take all this without it coming through the top of my skull? Was I setting myself up for death by fucking? I knew Bre's advice was gonna have me in over my damn head. But I couldn't exactly slide off without looking like a punk.

So, I did what I had to do, planting both feet firmly in the mattress on either side of his waist, gripping his dick like a microphone, and guiding it into my pussy carefully. As soon as the tip touched the lips of my pussy, my mouth flew open and Chad's knees knocked together. He leaned forward just enough to plant his hands at the base of my hips. There was no way in hell I was gonna take it all in that position. My ambition had finally met its match

"I got you." He said, holding me in place as he sat up and rested his back against the headboard. My eyes fell closed as he sank deeper inside, legs roped around his waist as I slid back and forth over his length.

And oh my God, he felt so good. Widening against my walls, stroking dangerously close to the spot that had been waiting there for him to touch since the last time he unraveled me. Had it not been for his fear of hurting me, he would've loosened his hold and plunged all the way in. But he was my lover and my protector, two lines that he was gonna have to learn to separate in the bedroom because a part of me that I never knew existed wanted the pain. Especially knowing that there was pleasure on the other side of it.

"Baby." I moaned into his ear, pressed flush against his chest, heart beating in sync with his as one of his hands gripped my ass.

I grinded against him, hips waving back and forth, covering and uncovering his erection like the sexiest magic trick. My head fell back as he pulled me harder against him, anchoring deep, deep inside me with his teeth sinking into my neck.

"Taya, shit!" He groaned, rocking against me harder, disregarding whatever restraint he'd been showing early on. Full to the brim with his flesh, I was. Pussy lips parting and slowly swelling. A sense of urgency had built at the pit of my stomach forcing me to reciprocate every one of his thrusts. I kept on sliding over him as hard and as fast as I could, panting and moaning and digging my nails in his back. His hold around my waist was the only anchor present or necessary while he plunged into the center of me, forcing all resistance to the ends of my limbs where they faded and fell onto the mattress.

I didn't have to feel this sensation more than once to know that I was about to melt into pieces. With Chad so big and deep inside me and him groaning against my neck, I swallowed my screams then let them out on an invisible ribbon that carried his name.

"Chad!" My head shot up to the ceiling, flashes of light forced my eyes open.

Once, twice, three times he pushed into me. And then there was no more to be claimed. Our bodies gave in to their undoing.

With no desire to be anywhere but where I was, my head collapsed on his shoulder, cheek wet from the sweat that had trickled down his neck. I kissed him there, indulging in the saltiness of his perspiration. I could feel his cheek raising against mine as he smiled. Thank God he was happy too.

"You still love me?" He asked, such a simple concern had me blushing on the inside and out.

"Yeah," I replied as if we'd had this exchange more than once.

"Good." He smiled. "Also, there's a big ass pair of shoes at the doorway. Any idea who they belong to?"

"Sabre," I replied without hesitation. "Bre doesn't think I saw him tiptoeing into her room like Santa on Christmas Eve. But this doorbell camera picks up everything and that's all I have to say about that."

Chad busted out laughing and dropped the whole subject, pulling my legs around him tighter as he flipped his legs off the side of the bed, then stood up and carried us both to the shower where he took his time and washed me clean.

The End…

Nasty (An Erotic Spin-Off)
Plus
The Fold Thou Shall Not Run (Book One)
Freaky Tales
Desdemona's Closet: A Christmas Tale

To the readers…
Thank you so much for taking the time to read this story.
I hope you enjoyed reading it as much as I enjoyed
writing it!
For more of my stories, please visit my author page
On Amazon Sabrina B. Scales
And please, rate and review.
It's the best gift any reader can leave for an author,
Worth more than its weight in gold!
For inquiries, please contact me at:
Sabrinabscales@gmail.com
Or
Like us on Facebook Author Sabrina B. Scales
Or
Join us in the bricks reading group
Or
Follow us on instagram @auhtorsabrinabscales
Thanks a bunch. Keep reading!